Joss knew what was coming. He was going to kiss her.

And oh, at that moment, she *wanted* him to kiss her.

Wanted him to guide her back onto the sofa cushions, to press his big, muscled body so tightly against her, to hold her so close and kiss her so long, and so deep and so thoroughly that she would forget…

Everything.

The mess that was her life. All the ways her plans and her world had gone haywire. All the things she somehow had to fix, to make right, though she really had no idea how to do that.

She wanted to tear off all her clothes and all of his, too. She wanted to be naked with him, skin-to-skin. Naked with her new best friend—who happened to be a man she'd only met the day before.

She wanted forgetfulness. And she wanted it in Jace's big arms.

Dear Reader,

Former player Jason "Jace" Traub isn't sure what he wants out of life anymore. He's out of the family business and determined to leave his lifelong home of Midland, Texas, and start anew somewhere else. In the meantime, he's spending a week or two at the annual Traub family reunion in Thunder Canyon, Montana.

Runaway bride Joss Bennings is enjoying her *un*-honeymoon at the Thunder Canyon Resort courtesy of that cheating rat she almost married. When Jace meets Joss, it's best friends at first sight.

Nothing serious. They're just great buddies.

Or so they keep telling themselves. But every moment they spend together draws them closer to the realization that there's a lot more going on there than friendship.

I love it when best friends become so much more. I think Joss and Jace are meant for each other. And I totally enjoyed writing their story.

Happy reading, everyone!

Yours always,

Christine Rimmer

THE LAST SINGLE MAVERICK

CHRISTINE RIMMER

Special thanks and acknowledgment to Christine Rimmer for her contribution to the Montana Mavericks: Back in the Saddle continuity.

ISBN-13: 978-0-373-65679-0

THE LAST SINGLE MAVERICK

This edition published by arrangement with Harlequin Books S.A.

For questions and comments about the quality of this book please contact us at Customer_eCare@Harlequin.ca.

www.Harlequin.com

Printed in U.S.A.

Books by Christine Rimmer

Harlequin Special Edition

¶¶*Resisting Mr. Tall, Dark & Texan* #2125
§*A Bravo Homecoming* #2150
§*The Return of Bowie Bravo* #2168
¤*The Last Single Maverick* #2197

Silhouette Special Edition

†*The Millionaire She Married* #1322
†*The M.D. She Had to Marry* #1345
The Tycoon's Instant Daughter #1369
†*The Marriage Agreement* #1412
†*The Marriage Conspiracy* #1423
***His Executive Sweetheart* #1485
***Mercury Rising* #1496
***Scrooge and the Single Girl* #1509
††*The Reluctant Princess* #1537
††*Prince and Future...Dad?* #1556
††*The Marriage Medallion* #1567
§*Fifty Ways to Say I'm Pregnant* #1615
§*Marrying Molly* #1639
§§*Stranded with the Groom* #1657
§*Lori's Little Secret* #1683
§*The Bravo Family Way* #1741
‡*The Reluctant Cinderella* #1765
§*Married in Haste* #1777
§*From Here to Paternity* #1825
‡‡*The Man Who Had Everything* #1837
§*A Bravo Christmas Reunion* #1868
§*Valentine's Secret Child* #1879
°*In Bed with the Boss* #1909
§*Having Tanner Bravo's Baby* #1927
§*The Stranger and Tessa Jones* #1945
§*The Bravo Bachelor* #1963
§*A Bravo's Honor* #1975
§*Christmas at Bravo Ridge* #2012
§*Valentine Bride* #2023
§*A Bride for Jericho Bravo* #2029
¶*McFarlane's Perfect Bride* #2053
§*Expecting the Boss's Baby* #2077
§*Donovan's Child* #2095
§*Marriage, Bravo Style!* #2101

Desire

No Turning Back #418
Call It Fate #458
Temporary Temptress #602
Hard Luck Lady #640
Midsummer Madness #729
Counterfeit Bride #812
Cat's Cradle #940
The Midnight Rider Takes A Bride #1101

Silhouette Books

Fortune's Children
Wife Wanted
**The Taming of Billy Jones*
†*The Bravo Billionaire*
Montana Mavericks: Big Sky Brides
"Suzanna"
Lone Star Country Club
Stroke of Fortune
Lone Star Country Club: The Debutantes
"Reinventing Mary"

Harlequin Books

Special Edition Bonus Story:
The Anniversary Party—Chapter Two

*The Jones Gang
†Conveniently Yours
**The Sons of Caitlin Bravo
††Viking Brides
§Bravo Family Ties
§§Montana Mavericks:
Gold Rush Grooms
‡Talk of the Neighborhood
‡‡Montana Mavericks: Striking It Rich
°Back in Business
¶Montana Mavericks:
Thunder Canyon Cowboys
¶¶Montana Mavericks:
The Texans Are Coming!
°°The Bravo Royales
¤Montana Mavericks:
Back in the Saddle

Other titles by this author
available in ebook format

CHRISTINE RIMMER

came to her profession the long way around. Before settling down to write about the magic of romance, she'd been everything from an actress to a salesclerk to a waitress. Now that she's finally found work that suits her perfectly, she insists she never had a problem keeping a job—she was merely gaining "life experience" for her future as a novelist. Christine is grateful not only for the joy she finds in writing, but for what waits when the day's work is through: a man she loves who loves her right back, and the privilege of watching their children grow and change day to day. She lives with her family in Oregon. Visit Christine at www.christinerimmer.com.

For my readers.
You are the best!

Chapter One

Family reunions. Who needs them?

Jason Traub didn't. He realized that now. And yet somehow, a few days ago, he'd decided that a trip to Montana for the annual summertime Traub family get-together would be a good idea.

Or maybe he'd just wanted to escape Midland, Texas, and the constant pressure to return to the family business. He should have realized that in Montana it would only be more of the same. Especially given that the whole family was here—and still putting on the pressure.

And why was it that the reunion seemed to get longer every year? This year, it began on the Saturday before Independence Day and would go straight through the whole week to the Sunday after the Fourth, with some family event or other taking place daily.

That first day, Saturday, June 30, featured a late-afternoon barbecue at DJ's Rib Shack. Jason's cousin DJ had Rib Shacks all over the western states. But this one happened to be at the Thunder Canyon Resort up on Thunder Mountain, which loomed, tall and craggy, above the small and charming mountain town of Thunder Canyon.

"Jace." The deep voice came from behind him. "Glad you could make it."

Jason, seated at one of the Rib Shack's long, rustic, family-style tables, glanced over his shoulder at his older brother Ethan. "Great party," Jason said. And it was. If you didn't mind a whole bunch of family up in your face in a big, big way.

His brother leaned closer. "We need to talk."

Jace pretended he didn't hear and held up a juicy rib dripping Rib Shack secret sauce. "Great ribs, as always." With the constant rumble of voices and laughter that filled the restaurant, how would Ethan know if Jace heard him or not?

Ethan grunted—and bent even closer to speak directly into his ear. "I know Ma and Pete want you back in Midland." Pete Wexler was their stepdad. "But you've got options, and I mean that. There's a place waiting for you right here at TOI Montana."

TOI—for Traub Oil Industries—was the family business. The original office was in Midland, Texas, where Jason and his five siblings had been born and raised. Pete, their stepdad, was chairman of the board. And their mother, Claudia, was CEO. Last year, Ethan had opened a second branch of TOI in Thunder Canyon. Jackson, Jason's fraternal twin, and their only sister, Rose, and her husband, Austin, were all at the new office with Ethan.

"No, thanks," Jace said, and then reminded his brother—as he kept reminding everyone in the family, "I'm out of the oil business."

Now it was Ethan's turn to pretend not to hear. He

squeezed Jason's shoulder—a bone-crushing squeeze. "We'll talk," he said.

"No point," Jace answered wearily. "I've made up my mind."

But Ethan only gave him a wave and started talking to the large elderly woman on Jace's right. Jace didn't hear what they said to each other. He was actively *not* listening.

A moment later, Ethan moved on. Jace concentrated on his dinner. His plate was piled high with ribs, corn on the cob, coleslaw and steak fries. The food was terrific. Almost worth the constant grief he was getting from his family—about work, about his nonexistent love life, about *everything.*

Across the table, Shandie Traub, his cousin Dax's wife, said, "Jason, here's someone I want you to meet." The someone in question stood directly behind Shandie. She had baby-fine blond hair and blue eyes and she was smiling at him shyly. Shandie introduced her. "My second cousin, Belinda McKelly. Belinda's from Sioux Falls."

"Hi, Jason." Belinda colored prettily. She had to practically shout to be heard over the din. "I'm so pleased to meet you." She bent closer and stuck her hand out at him.

Jace swiped a wet wipe over his fingers, reached across the table and gave her offered hand a shake. She seemed sweet actually. But one look in those baby blues of hers told him way more than he needed to know: Belinda wanted a husband. As soon as she let go, he grabbed an ear of corn and started gnawing on it, his gaze focused hard on his plate. When he dared to glance up again, she was gone.

Shandie gave him a look that skimmed real close to pissed off. "Honestly, Jace, you could make a little effort. It's not like it would kill you."

"Sorry," he said, even though he didn't feel sorry in the

least. He only felt relieved not to have to make small talk with sweet Belinda McKelly.

To his right, the large elderly woman Ethan had spoken to a few moments before said warmly, "Such a lovely young girl." The old lady's warm tone turned cool as she spoke directly to Jason. "But I can see *you're* not interested." He kept working away at his ear of corn in hopes that the large old lady would turn and talk to the smaller old lady on her other side. No such luck. "I'm Melba Landry," she said, "Lizzie's great-aunt." Lizzie was Ethan's wife.

Resigned, Jason gave the woman a nod. "Pleased to meet you, ma'am. I'm Jason Traub, Lizzie's brother-in-law."

"I know very well who you are, young man." Aunt Melba looked down her imposing nose at him. "I was married to Lizzie's great-uncle Oliver for more than fifty years. Oliver, rest his soul, passed on last October. The Lord never saw fit to bless us with children of our own. I moved to Thunder Canyon just this past April. It's so nice to be near Lizzie. Family is everything, don't you think, Jason?"

"Yes, ma'am. Everything." To his left, he was vaguely aware that the second cousin sitting there had risen. Someone else slipped into the empty spot.

And Aunt Melba wasn't through with him yet. "Jason, you know that we're all *concerned* about you."

"Kind of seems that way, yes." He got busy on his second ear of corn, still hoping that putting all his attention on the food would get rid of her. It had worked with Belinda.

But Aunt Melba was not about to give up. "I understand you're having some kind of life crisis."

He swallowed. The wad of corn went down hard. He grabbed his water glass and knocked back a giant gulp. "Life crisis? No, ma'am. I'm not."

"Please call me Melba—and there's no point in lying

about it. I'm seventy-six years old, young man. I know a man in crisis when I see one."

"No, ma'am," he said again. "I mean that. There's no crisis." By then, he was starting to feel a little like Judas at the last supper. If he just kept denying, maybe she would go away.

"I asked you to call me Melba," she corrected a second time, more sternly.

"Sorry, Melba. But I mean it. I'm not having a crisis. I am doing just fine. And really, I—"

"There's a lovely church here in town that I've been attending. Everyone is so friendly. I felt at home there from the first. And so will you, Jason."

"Uh…"

"Tomorrow. Join us. The Thunder Canyon Community Church. North Main at Cedar Street. Come to the service at ten. I'll be watching for you. There is no problem in this wide world that a little time with the Lord can't resolve."

"Well, Melba, thank you for the invitation. I'll, um, try to be there."

"Get involved, young man," Melba instructed with an enthusiastic nod of her imposing double chin. "That's the first step. Stop sitting on the sidelines of life." She opened her mouth to say more, but the white-haired lady on her other side touched her arm and spoke to her. Melba turned to answer.

Jace held his breath. And luck was with him. Melba and the other old lady had struck up a conversation.

He was just starting to feel relieved when a hand closed on his left thigh and a sultry voice spoke in his ear. "Jace, aren't you even going to say hi?"

He smelled musky perfume and turned his head slowly to meet a pair of glittering green eyes. "Hi."

The woman was not any member of his extended family

that he knew of. She had jet-black hair and wore a painted-on red tank top. "Oh, you're kidding me." She laughed. "You don't remember? Last summer? Your brother Corey's bachelor party at the Hitching Post?" The Hitching Post was a landmark restaurant and bar in town.

"I, uh..."

"Theresa," the woman said. "Theresa Duvall."

"Hey." He tried on a smile. He remembered her now—vaguely anyway. For Jace, the weekend of Corey's bachelor party and wedding had been mostly of the "lost" variety. His twin, Jackson, had still been single then. The two of them had partied straight through for three days. There had been serious drinking. Way too much drinking. And the night of the bachelor party, he'd gone home with Theresa, hadn't he? Somehow, that had seemed like a good idea at the time. "So, Theresa," he said, "how've you been?"

Her hand glided a little higher on his thigh. "I have been fine, Jace. Just fine. And it is so *good* to see you," she cooed. "I had *such* a great time with you." Theresa, as he recalled, was not the least interested in settling down. In fact, the look on her face told him exactly what she *was* interested in: another night like that one last summer.

He *had* to get out of there. He grabbed another wipe, swabbed off his greasy fingers and then gently removed Theresa's wandering hand from his thigh. "Excuse me, Theresa."

"Oh, now," she coaxed in a breathy whisper, "don't run off."

"Men's room?" He put a question mark after it, even though he knew perfectly well where the restrooms were.

Theresa pointed. "Over there." She gave him a low-eyed, smoldering glance as he pushed his chair out and rose. "Hurry back," she instructed, licking her lips.

It wasn't easy, but he forced himself not to take off at

a run. He ambled away casually, waving and nodding to friends and family as he headed for the restrooms—only detouring sharply for the exit as soon as he was no longer in Theresa's line of sight. A moment later, he ducked out of the Rib Shack altogether and into the giant, five-story clubhouse lobby of the resort.

Now what?

Someplace quiet. Someplace where he could be alone.

The Lounge, he thought. It was a bar in the clubhouse and it was exactly what he needed right now. The Lounge was kind of a throwback really—a throwback to earlier times, when cattlemen had their own private clubs where the women didn't trespass. In the Lounge, the lights were kept soothingly low. The bar was long and made of gleaming burled wood. It had comfortable conversation areas consisting of dark wood tables and fat studded-leather chairs. Women seemed to avoid the Lounge. They tended to prefer the more open, modern bar in the upscale Gallatin Room, or the cowboy-casual style of the bar in the Rib Shack.

The Lounge was perfect for the mood he was in.

He found it as he'd hoped it might be—mostly deserted. One lone customer sat up at the bar. A woman, surprisingly enough. A brunette. Jace liked the look of her instantly, which surprised him. As a rule lately, it didn't matter how hot or good-looking a woman was. He just wasn't interested. Not on any level.

But *this* woman was different. Special. He sensed that at first sight.

She had a whole lot of thick, tousled brown hair tumbling down her back. In the mirror over the bar, he could see that she had big brown eyes and full, kissable lips. She was dressed casually, in jeans and a giant white shirt, untucked. She wore very little makeup.

And the best thing about her? She seemed so relaxed. Like she wasn't after anything except to sip her margarita and enjoy the quiet comfort of the Lounge.

She saw him watching her in the mirror over the bar. For a second or two, their eyes met. He felt a little curl of excitement down inside him before she glanced away. Instantly, he wanted her to glance at him again.

Surprise. Excitement. The desire that a certain woman might give him a second look. These were all emotions with which he'd become completely unfamiliar.

Yeah, all right. It wasn't news that he used to be something of a player. But in the past six months or so? Uh-uh. He was tired of being a ladies' man—like he was tired of just about everything lately. Including finding the right woman and settling down.

Because, yeah, Jason had tried that. Or at least, he'd wanted to try it with a certain rich-girl swimsuit model named Tricia Lavelle.

It hadn't worked out. In fact, the whole experience had been seriously disheartening.

A cell phone on the bar started ringing. The brunette picked it up, scowled at the display and then put it to her ear. "What do you want?" She let out an audible sigh. "You're not serious. Oh, please, Kenny, get real. It's over. Move on." She hung up and dropped the phone back on the bar.

Jace took the stool next to her and signaled the bartender. "Jack Daniels, rocks." The bartender poured and set his drink in front of him. "And another margarita," Jace added. "For the lady."

"No, thanks." She shook her head at the barkeep and he left them alone. Then she turned to Jace and granted him a patient look from that fine pair of enormous brown eyes. "No offense," she said.

"None taken."

"And don't even *think* about it, okay? I'm on a solo vacation and right now, I hate men."

He studied her face. It was such a great face. One of those faces a guy could look at forever and still find new expressions in it. "Already, I really like you."

"Didn't I just say I hate men?"

"That makes you a challenge. Haven't you heard? Men love a challenge."

"I'm serious. Don't bother. It's not gonna happen."

He faced the rows of liquor bottles arrayed in front of the mirror over the bar and shrugged. "Okay, if you're sure."

She shot him a look. "Oh, come on. Is that the best you've got?"

He leaned his head on his hand and admired the way the dim barroom light somehow managed to bring out glints of auburn in her thick, wavy dark hair. "Uninspired, huh?"

She almost smiled. "Well, yeah."

"Story of my life lately. I've got no passion for the game."

"What game?"

He shrugged again. "Any game."

She considered that. "Wow," she said finally. "That's sad."

"Yeah, it is, isn't it?"

She frowned and then looked at him sideways. "Wait a minute. Stop right there, buddy. I'm on to you."

"Oh? What am I up to?"

"You sit there looking gorgeous and bored. I find I have a longing to bring some life back into your eyes. I let you buy me another margarita after all. I go home with you. We have wild, hot, incredible sex. But in the morning, you're looking bored again and I'm feeling cheap and used."

He decided to focus on the positive. "You think I'm gorgeous?"

"That was not my point. It was a cautionary tale."

"I think *you're* gorgeous," he said and meant it. "And that's kind of a breakthrough for me."

"A breakthrough." She was not impressed. "You're kidding me."

"I am as serious as a bad blind date. You're the first woman I've felt attracted to in months. Who's Kenny?"

She shook a finger at him. "You listened in on my phone call."

"Not exactly. I *overheard* your phone call."

"I'm just saying it was a private conversation and I don't even know your name."

"Jason Traub. Call me Jace." He offered his hand.

She took it. "Jocelyn Marie Bennings. Call me Joss."

It felt good, he realized, just to hold her hand. It felt… comfortable. And exciting, too. Both at once. That was a first—for him anyway. As a rule, with women, it was one or the other. He didn't want to let go. But in the end, it wasn't his choice.

She eased her hand free. "My wedding was supposed to be a week ago today. Kenny was the groom."

"Supposed to be? You mean you *didn't* marry him?"

"No, I didn't. And I should have backed out long before the wedding day. But Kenny and I were together for five years. It was going to be a beautiful wedding. You should see my wedding gown. I still have it. I couldn't bear to get rid of it. It's fabulous. Acres of beading, yards of the finest taffeta and tulle. We planned a nice reception afterward at my restaurant."

"You own a restaurant?"

"No. I mean the restaurant I was managing, until I quit to marry Kenny. I gave up a great job for him. Just like I gave up my cute apartment, because I thought I wouldn't need either anymore."

"But then you didn't marry Kenny."

"I already said I didn't."

"Just wanted to be sure. So what went wrong? Why didn't you marry the guy?"

She ran her finger around the rim of her margarita glass. "Who's telling this story, Jace?"

He gave her a nod. "You are, Joss. Absolutely. Carry on."

"It was going to be the perfect wedding."

He nodded once more, to show her he was listening, but he did not interrupt again.

She went on. "And after the wedding and the lovely reception, there was the great getaway honeymoon right here at the Thunder Canyon Resort. Followed by a move to San Francisco. Kenny's a very successful advertising executive. He just hit the big time and got transferred to the Bay Area." Joss paused. She turned her glass by the stem.

He wanted to prompt her to tell him what went wrong, but he didn't. He waited patiently for her to go on, as he'd promised he would.

Finally, she continued. "I got all the way to the church last Saturday. Camellia City Methodist in Sacramento. It's a beautiful church. And I was born and raised in Sacramento and have lived there all my life. I like my hometown. In fact, I didn't really want to move to San Francisco, but I was willing to support my future husband in his powerhouse career. And I would have gone through with the wedding in spite of my doubts."

He'd promised to let her tell it her way, but still. He had to know. "What doubts?"

She shook her head. "Kenny used to be such a sweet guy. But the more successful he got, the more he changed.

He became someone I didn't even know—and then I caught him with my cousin Kimberly in the coat room."

"Hold on, you lost me. What coat room?"

She shook her head again, as though she still couldn't quite believe it. "The coat room at Camellia City Methodist."

Jace let his mouth fall open. "Kenny canoodled with Kimberly in the coat room on the day of your wedding?"

"Oh, yeah. And it was beyond canoodling. Kimberly was halfway out of her hot-pink satin bridesmaid's dress and someone had unzipped Kenny's fly. Both of them were red-faced and breathless. Kind of ruined the whole experience for me, you know?"

He made a low noise in his throat. "I guess so."

Joss picked up the cell phone, studied it for a moment and then set it back down. "So I threw his engagement ring in his face and got the heck out of there—and I'm here at the resort anyway. Having my honeymoon minus the groom."

He tipped his head at the phone. "But Kenny keeps calling."

"Oh yes, he does."

"What a douche bag."

She sipped her margarita. "My sentiments exactly."

"I hate guys like that. He blew it already. He should show a little dignity and leave you alone. But instead it's, 'Joss, *please*. I love you. I just want to work this out. Come back to me. I'm sorry, okay? And that silly thing with Kimberly? It meant nothing and it will never happen again.'"

Joss laughed. She had a beautiful, husky, warm sort of laugh. "How did you do that? You even captured the slightly wounded, whiney tone of his voice. Like *I'm* the one with the problem."

Jace stared at her wide, soft mouth in unabashed admiration. "I like your laugh."

She gave him her sternest frown. "Didn't I tell you not to go there?"

He was about to argue that he wasn't "going" anywhere, that he only liked the way she laughed. But before he could get the words out, Theresa Duvall sauntered up behind him and took the stool on his other side.

"Jace." Theresa's hand closed over his arm. He looked down at her fingernails, which were long and done up for the holiday with glittery red stripes and tiny, sparkly little stars. She leaned close and purred, "I'm a determined woman and there is no way you're escaping me."

Okay. He knew he only had himself to blame if Theresa considered him the perfect candidate for another no-strings night of meaningless sex. But he really liked Joss. And he'd never have a chance with her now, not with Theresa pulling on his arm, eyeing him like a starving person eyes a steak dinner.

And it wasn't even that he *wanted* a chance with Joss. Not *that* kind of chance anyway. He just liked her a lot, liked talking with her, liked hearing her laugh. He didn't want her to leave.

Shocked the socks off him when she *didn't* leave. Somehow, she picked up on the desperate look he sent her. And not only did she stay right where she was, she wrapped her arm around his shoulders and pulled him away from Theresa, drawing him close to her side.

Wow. It felt good—*really* good—to have her holding on to him, to feel her softness and the warmth of her. She smelled like soap and starch and sunshine and roses. And maybe a little tequila.

"Sorry," she said to Theresa, her tone regretful. "This one's taken."

Theresa blinked. And then she let go of his arm and scowled. "Jace, what *is* your problem? You should have told me you were with someone. I want a good time as much as the next girl, but I would never steal another woman's man."

He was totally lost, awash in the superfine sensation of having Joss's arm around him. But then she nudged him in the side and he realized he was supposed to speak. "Uh, yeah. You're right, Theresa. I'm an ass. I should have said something."

Joss clucked her tongue and rolled her eyes. "We had a fight. He's been sulking."

Theresa groaned. "Oh, I know how that goes. Men. I don't let myself get serious with them anymore. They're just not worth it."

Joss pulled him even closer. And then she kissed his ear. It was barely a breath of a kiss. But still, with her arm around him and her lips close to his ear, he could almost forget that he had no interest in women anymore. He was enjoying every minute of this and he wished she would never let go. "I hear you," she told Theresa, her breath all warm and tempting in his ear. "But when it's true love, well, what can you do?"

Theresa just shook her head. The bartender approached. Theresa shook her head at him, too. And then, without another word, she got up and left.

Instantly, Joss released him and retreated to her own stool. Jace felt kind of bereft. But then he reminded himself that he should be grateful. She'd done him a favor and gotten Theresa off his back. "Thanks. I owe you one." He raised his glass.

She tapped hers against it. "Okay, I'll bite. Who *was* that?"

"Her name is Theresa Duvall. Last year, she was working at the Hitching Post—it's this great old-time bar and grill down in town, on the corner of Main Street and Thunder Canyon Road."

"She seemed like she knew you pretty well."

"Not really." He didn't want to say more. But Joss was looking at him, a look that seemed to expect him to tell the truth. So he did. "I had a thing with her last summer. A very short thing."

"A thing."

"Yeah."

"What, specifically, is a thing?"

He tried not to wince. "See, I knew you would ask that."

Joss accused gently, "You slept with her."

"Only once. And technically, well, there was no sleeping."

She laughed again. Really, she had the best laugh. "Jace, I believe you're a dog."

He tipped his drink and stared down into it. "Maybe I was. Not anymore, though. I have changed my ways."

She made a disbelieving sound. "Right."

"No, seriously, I'm not the man I used to be. Too bad I'm not real clear on who, exactly, I've become. I lack… direction. Everyone says so. I'm not interested in women anymore. I don't want to get laid. Or married. Also, I've given up my place in the family business and my family is freaked over that."

"You live here in Thunder Canyon?"

"No, in Midland, Texas. Or I did. I have a nice little spread outside of town there. But I've put my place up for sale. I'm moving. I just don't know where to yet. In the meantime, I'm here for a weeklong family reunion—a reunion that is going on right now, here at the resort, over at DJ's Rib Shack."

"I have another question, Jace."

"Shoot."

"Is there anything you *do* want?"

"That, Jocelyn Marie, is the question of the hour. Please come with me back to the Rib Shack."

She was running her finger around the rim of her drink again. "You didn't answer the question of the hour."

"All right. There is nothing that I want—except for you to come back to the Rib Shack with me."

Her smooth brow furrowed a little. "And *I* would want to go to *your* family reunion because?"

"Because only you can protect me from my family and all the women who want things from me that I'm not capable of giving them."

She shook that head of thick brown hair and sat straighter on her stool. "Before I decide whether to go with you or not, I need to get something crystal clear."

"Fine."

"I want you to listen very carefully, Jace."

He assumed a suitably intent expression. "I'm listening."

"I'm. Not. Going. To. Have. Sex. With. You."

"Oh, that." He waved a hand. "It's okay. I don't care about that."

"So you say now."

"Look, Joss, I like you. You're the first bright spot in my life in months. I just want to hang around with you for a while. Have a few laughs. No pressure. No drama. Nothing hot and heavy. No big romance."

She stared at him for several seconds. Her expression said she still wasn't sure she believed him. Finally she asked, "So you want to be…friends? Honestly? Just friends?"

"My God, I would love that." He put some money on the bar. "The Rib Shack?"

She downed the last of her margarita. "Why not?"

Chapter Two

Joss surprised herself when she agreed to go with Jace.

But then, she got what he meant when he said that he *liked* her. She liked him, too. And not because he was tall and lean and handsome with thick, glossy dark hair and velvet-brown eyes. Not because he smelled of soap and a nice, clean, subtle, probably very expensive aftershave. Not because he was undeniably hot.

She didn't care about hot. Her life had pretty much crumbled to nothing a week before. Finding a hot guy—or any guy for that matter— was the last thing on her mind.

Jocelyn liked Jason because he made her laugh. Because, even though he carried himself like he owned the world, she could see in his eyes that he really was flummoxed by life, that he used to be one guy and now he wasn't that guy anymore. That he wasn't all that familiar with the guy he was now. Joss could relate to that kind of confusion. It was exactly the confusion she felt.

She entered the Rib Shack on Jace's arm. The casual, Western-themed restaurant was packed. Jason Traub, as it turned out, had a very large family.

"Jason, there you are," said a good-looking older woman with a slim figure and sleek light brown hair. "I was starting to wonder if you'd already left."

"No, Ma," Jace said, his charming smile not quite masking the wariness in his eyes. "I'm still here."

Jace's mother turned a bright glance on Joss. "Hello."

Jace made the introductions. Joss smiled and nodded at his mom, whose name was Claudia.

Claudia asked, "Do you live here in town, Jocelyn?"

"No, I'm from Sacramento."

Jace said, "Joss is staying here at the resort."

"With your family?" his mom quizzed. Claudia had that look, Joss thought, the look of a mother on the trail of every bit of information she could gather about the new girl her son had brought to the family party.

"I'm here on my own," Joss told her. "Having a great time, too. I love the spa. And the shopping in the resort boutiques. And I'm learning to play golf." All of it on Kenny Donovan's dime, thank you very much.

An ordinary-looking man a few years older than Jace's mom stepped up and took Claudia's arm. Claudia beamed at him, her golden-brown eyes glowing with affection. "Darling, this is Jocelyn, Jason's new friend. Jocelyn, my husband, Pete—we're staying here at the resort, too. A romantic getaway, just us two old folks in the Governor's Suite."

Joss was in the Honeymoon Suite, but she didn't say so. It would only be asking for more questions than she was prepared to answer at the moment—which was kind of amusing in a dark sort of way. She hadn't even hesitated to tell Jace that she'd run away from her own wedding. But somehow, with everyone else, well, she didn't want to go there. And she really appreciated that Jace was keeping his mouth shut about it.

He seemed like a great guy. And his parents were adorable, she thought. So much in love, so attentive to each other. There should be more couples in the world like Claudia and Pete.

Claudia said, "I hope you'll join us for dinner tomorrow night, Jocelyn. It will be at the home of Jason's twin, Jackson, and Jackson's wife, Laila. They have a nice little property not far from town."

"Yeah, you should come," Jace said with enthusiasm. "I'll take you."

Joss gave him a look that said he shouldn't push it and asked, "You have a twin?"

Claudia laughed. "A fraternal twin. Jackson is older by an hour and five minutes. That makes Jason my youngest son. I also have one daughter, Rose. She's the baby of the family. Dillon, Ethan and Corey are the older boys."

Joss did the math. "Wow, six kids. I'm jealous. I was an only child. My mother raised me on her own."

Claudia reached out and touched Joss's shoulder, a fond kind of touch. "Sweet girl," she said softly. And Joss felt all warm and fuzzy inside. "You come to dinner tomorrow night," Jace's mom said again. "We would love to have you join us."

"Thank you," Joss said, and left it at that.

A few moments later, Jace led her out onto the Rib Shack's patio where the band was set up but taking a break. They found a reasonably quiet corner where they could talk without having to shout.

"My mother likes you," Jace said.

"You say that like you're not sure if it's good or bad."

"Yeah, well, Ma thinks I got my heart broken and she

really wants me to be happy. She's decided I only need to meet another woman, the *right* woman, so I can get married and settle down like my brothers and my sister. Now she'll be finding all kinds of ways to throw us together."

"We'll resist, of course."

"Of course we will."

"Who broke your heart, Jace?"

He hedged. "It's a long story."

"I told you mine," she teased.

He looked distinctly uncomfortable. "Well, you know, this isn't the place or the time."

She got the message. "You don't want to tell me—and you know what? That's okay."

"Whew." He made a show of wiping nonexistent sweat from his brow. "And even though I hate to give my mother the wrong idea about us, I think you ought to come to dinner at Jackson's tomorrow. You know, just to be social."

She gave him a slow look. She knew he was up to something.

And he was. He admitted, "I also want you there because I like you."

"Uh-huh. What else? Give it to me straight, Jace."

"Fair enough. If you come, everyone will think we're together—I mean *really* together, as in more than friends. And that means my family will stop trying to set me up."

"You want me to pretend to be your girlfriend?"

"You don't have to pretend anything. If you're with me, they'll assume there's something going on. It doesn't matter if you tell them that we're just friends. They won't believe you. It doesn't matter that *I* will tell them we're just friends. They'll only be certain we're in denial about all that we mean to each other."

"Still, it seems dishonest."

"Is it our fault if people insist on jumping to conclusions?"

Strangely, she found that she *wanted* to go to dinner at his brother's house. "I'll think about it."

"Good. And don't let my mother get you alone. She'll only start in about the family business and how she needs me in Midland and she hopes that *you* will be open to the idea of moving to Texas because she's already hearing wedding bells in our future."

"What *is* the family business anyway?"

"I didn't tell you? It's oil. Except for my oldest brother, Dillon, who's a doctor, we're all in oil."

She laughed. "Knee-deep?"

"All the way over our heads in it, trust me. We're Traub Oil Industries. I was a vice president in the Midland office. I quit the first of April. I was supposed to be out of there by the end of May. My mother and Pete kept finding reasons why I had to stay. I finally escaped just this past Wednesday. I'm never going back."

"You sound determined."

"Believe me, I am."

"How come you call your dad Pete?"

"He's my stepdad. My father, Charles, was something of a legend in the oil business. He died in an accident on a rig when I was little. My mom married Pete about two years later. Her last name is Wexler now. None of us were happy when she married him. We were loyal to our dad and we resented Pete."

"We?"

"My brothers, my sister and I. But Pete's not only a good man, he's also a patient one. He won all of us over eventually. Pete had a heart attack a couple of years ago. We almost lost him. That really taught us how much he means to us."

"It's so obvious he's head over heels in love with your mom."

"Yes, he is. A man like that is damn hard to hate." He took her arm. "Come on, I want you to meet my brothers."

They wandered back inside. Joss met Dillon and Ethan and Corey and Jace's twin, Jackson. The two did look a lot alike—meaning tall, dark and handsome. But it wasn't the least difficult to tell them apart. Joss also met the Traub boys' only sister, Rose, and Rose's husband, Austin, and she visited with the wives of Jason's brothers. She liked them all, with Lizzie, Ethan's wife, possibly being her favorite.

Lizzie Traub was tall and sturdily built, with slightly wild-looking dark blond hair and a no-nonsense way about her. She owned a bakery, the Mountain Bluebell, in town. Everyone said that Lizzie baked the best muffins in Montana.

And beyond Jace's brothers and sister and their spouses, there were Traub cousins, too: DJ and Dax and their wives Allaire and Shandie. And also Clay and Forrest Traub, two cowboys from Rust Creek Falls, which was about three hundred miles from Thunder Canyon.

Joss was starting to wonder how she was going to keep all their names straight when a woman named Melba Landry, who was Lizzie Traub's great-aunt, caught up with them. A big woman with a stern face, Melba possessed a truly impressive bosom. Joss tried not to laugh as the energetic old woman cornered Jace and insisted she wanted to see him at her church the next morning.

"Of course he'll come," Joss told Melba. "There's nothing Jace enjoys more than a good Sunday service."

Beside her, Jace made a low groaning sound.

And Melba turned her sharp hazel eyes on Joss. "Excellent. I want to see you there, too, young lady."

"Well, now, I don't exactly know if I—"

"We'll be there," Jace promised. Joss elbowed him in the ribs, but he didn't relent.

Aunt Melba said, "Wonderful. The service begins at ten." And she sailed off to corner some other unsuspecting potential churchgoer.

The party continued. It really was fun. Joss forgot her troubles and just had a good time. She spotted Theresa Duvall dancing with a tall, lean cowboy, one of Jace's cousins from Rust Creek Falls. Theresa clung to that cowboy like paint. She didn't seem the least upset that things hadn't worked out for her with Jace.

Joss and Jace danced. He was a good dancer. Plus, he kept to their agreement about just being friends. He didn't hold her too close. She swayed in his arms and thought how good it felt to be held by him. His body and hers just kind of fit together. He was a great guy and if things were different she would definitely be attracted to him. Really, the longer they danced, the more she started thinking that she wouldn't mind at all if he did hold her closer….

But no. That wouldn't be a good idea. The last thing she needed right now was a new man in her life. She liked Jace as a person, but still. He *was* a man. All man. And she wasn't trusting any man. Not now.

Not for a long, long time, if ever.

It was after ten when the party broke up. She and Jace were among the last to leave. They wandered out to the lobby together and then kind of naturally turned for the elevators side-by-side.

The Honeymoon Suite was on the top floor. The doors opened and they left the elevator.

At the door, she paused, key card in hand. "If I let you in, you have to promise not to put a move on me."

He looked hurt. "Joss, come on. How many ways can

I tell you? I need a friend. You need a friend. That's what we've got going on here. It's *all* we've got going on here."

She chewed her lower lip for a moment. "All right. I believe you." And then she stuck her key in the slot and pushed the door wide.

He followed her in, through the skylit foyer area into the living/dining room, which had floor-to-ceiling windows with a spectacular view. "Nice."

"Hey, only the best for Kenny Donovan's runaway bride." She headed for the wet bar. "How about a little champagne and caviar? On Kenny, of course."

"Got a beer?"

She gave him one from the fridge and grabbed a ginger ale for herself. "Make yourself at home." He took a fat leather easy chair and she shucked off her shoes and curled up on the sofa.

And they talked. About his family. About the party at the Rib Shack. About how they both thought Lizzie was great and how Lizzie's aunt Melba cracked them up.

"So how long are you here for?" he asked.

She thought how much she liked his voice. It was deep and warm and made her want to cuddle up against him—which she was *not*, under any circumstances, going to do. Ever. "Another week. As long as Kenny doesn't put a stop on his platinum card, I am having my whole two-week un-honeymoon."

"And then?"

"Back to Sacramento. To find a job. And a new place to live."

"We have so much in common," he said. "I'm here for a week, too."

"You told me. The family reunion. And then after that?"

"I suppose I'll have to get a life. But I'm not even going to think about that yet."

"Jace, I like the way you completely avoid anything remotely resembling responsibility. Aunt Melba would *so* not approve."

"Thank you, Joss. I do my best." He tipped his longneck at her. "I'm glad we're friends. Let's be *best* friends."

"All right. I'm up for that."

"Best friends for a week," he declared.

She held up her index finger and reminded him, "No benefits."

He looked at her from under his thick dark brows. "You know you're killin' me here. Have I, in any way, put any kind of move on you?"

"Nope, not a one."

"Then can we be done with the constant reminders about how I'm not supposed to try and get you naked?"

She saluted him with a hand to her forehead. "You got it. I believe you. You are not going to make any attempt whatsoever to get into my pants. Even if you *are* a man."

"Your trust is deeply touching."

The phone rang. It was on the side table next to the sofa, so she reached over and picked it up. "What?"

"Jocelyn, honestly. Is that any way to answer the phone?"

Without even thinking about it, Joss lowered her feet to the rug and sat up straighter. "Mom, hey." She ran a hand back through her hair. "What's up?"

"How can you ask me that? You know I'm worried sick about you."

"I'm fine. Really. Don't worry."

"When are you coming home?"

"I told you. A week from tomorrow." She sent Jace a sheepish glance and mouthed the word *Sorry.*

He shrugged to let her know it wasn't a big deal. Then he got up and went over to the wall of windows. He stood gazing out. She indulged in a long, slow look at him, from his fancy tooled boots, up over his lean legs and hips in crisp denim, his wide shoulders in a beautifully tailored midnight-blue Western shirt. His hair was thick and dark. She had no doubt it would be silky to the touch.

A great-looking guy. And a considerate one. It was kind of him to pretend to admire the view to give her the space she needed to take this unwelcome call. There ought to be more guys in the world like him.

Her mom said, "This is all just a big misunderstanding. You realize that, don't you? Kenny would never—"

"Mom." She struggled to keep her voice calm and even. "I *saw* him with Kimberly. There was no misunderstanding what I saw."

"Kimberly is terribly upset, too. She's hurt you would think such horrible, cruel things about her."

"Oh, please. Don't get me started on Kimberly. I don't want to talk about this anymore, Mom. I really don't."

"Kenny came to see me this evening."

Joss gasped. "He *what*?" She must have said it kind of loud because Jace glanced back at her, those sexy dark eyes full of concern. She shook her head at him. He turned to face the window again and she told her mother, "He has no right to bother you. None. Ever again."

"Honey, he's not bothering me. He loves you. He wants to work things out with you. He's crushed that you left him at the altar the way you did. You've humiliated him, but still, he forgives you and only wants to work things out so you two can be together as you were meant to be."

There was a crystal bowl full of expensive chocolates on the coffee table. Joss resisted the blinding urge to grab it and fling it at the far wall. "Mom, listen. Listen carefully. I am not going to get back together with Kenny. Ever. He and I are done. Finished. As over as it gets."

"If only your father hadn't left us. You wouldn't be so mistrustful of men. You wouldn't ruin the best chance you're ever going to get with a good man who will give you the kind of life you deserve."

She replied through clenched teeth. "There are so many ways I don't know how to respond to that."

"Just come home, honey. Come home right away."

"Mom, I'm hanging up now. I love you very much and I'll be home in a week."

"Jocelyn. Jocelyn, wait…"

But Joss didn't wait. She hung up the phone. And then she stared at it hard, *daring* it to ring again.

But apparently, her mother had come to her senses at least minimally and decided to leave awful enough alone.

For tonight anyway.

At the window, Jace turned. "Bad?"

She covered her face with her hands. "Yeah, beyond bad."

He left the window and came to her, walking softly in those fancy boots of his. She only heard his approach because she was listening for it. "Want to talk about it?"

"Ugh."

"Come on."

She lowered her hands and met his waiting eyes. He was standing across the coffee table from her, his hands in his pockets, accepting of whatever she might say, willing to listen. Ready to understand. She tipped her head at the cushion beside her. He took her invitation, crossing around the low table, dropping down next to her, stretching his arm out along the back of the couch in an invitation of his own.

An invitation she couldn't pass up at that moment. With a sad little sigh, she leaned her head on his shoulder. He smoothed her hair, but only lightly, and then draped his big arm around her.

It was a nice moment. Comforting. He was so large and warm and solid. And he smelled so clean and manly. And she really needed a strong shoulder to lean on. Just for a minute or two.

She said, "That was my mom."

"Yeah, I got that much."

"I told you she raised me on her own, didn't I?"

"You mentioned that, yeah."

"My dad disappeared when I was two. My mom says he just told her he was through one day and walked out. We never heard from him again."

"That's rough, Joss. Really rough." He squeezed her shoulder, a touch that comforted, that seemed to acknowledge how hard it had been for her. "It can really mess with your mind, to lose your dad when you're only a kid. It can leave you feeling like you're on the outside looking in—at all your friends and their happy, *whole* families. You grow up knowing what normal is. It's what all the *other* kids have."

She realized he was speaking from personal experience. "How old were you when your dad died?"

"Jackson and I were six."

"So at least you knew him, your dad."

"Kind of. He was always working, making his mark on the world, you could say. But yeah, we all looked up to him with stars in our eyes. We felt safe, just knowing he was our dad. He was one of those guys who really fills up a room. Rose always claims it was worse for her than for us boys. She never knew him—well, at least she doesn't remember him. She was two when he was killed."

"Same age I was when my dad left. And I don't remember him either. All I have is the…absence of him."

She pulled away enough to meet Jace's eyes. "You really don't need to hear this. You're sweet to be so understanding, but it's old news and it's got nothing to do with you."

He reached for her, pulled her back down to him. She started to resist, but then, well, why not, if he was willing to listen? She gave in and sagged against him, settling her head against his shoulder again—and yeah, she'd promised herself she would never cuddle up with him. But this wasn't cuddling. This was only leaning. And there was nothing wrong with a little leaning when a girl needed comfort from a friend.

"Keep talkin'," he said. "What's your mom's name?"

"RaeEllen. Her maiden name was Louvacek, but she kept my father's name, never changed it back. She always said she only wanted a good guy to stand by her. But I don't think she went looking after my dad left. It was like she...gave up when it came to men. She never dated when I was growing up, not that I can remember. She worked at Safeway, eventually moving up to managing her own store, which she still does to this day. And she took care of me. She was a good mom, a strict mom. And she always wanted the best for me. To her, Kenny seemed like a dream come true."

"So for some reason, she decided she could trust the cheater?"

"He was always good to her—kissing up to her really, it seems to me, in hindsight. When she would have us over for dinner, he would bring her flowers every time and fall all over her praising her cooking. And she knew how well he was doing at work, getting promotions, one after the other. She just...bought Kenny's act, hook, line and sinker. She refuses to believe that the thing with Kimberly even happened. Kenny's convinced her that I've blown an 'innocent encounter' all out of proportion."

"Convinced her? You're saying she's *speaking* to him, after what he did to you?"

"Because she doesn't believe he did anything bad, I guess she figures she's got no reason *not* to speak to him."

"She's your mom and I won't speak ill of her. But I will say she ought to get her loyalties straight."

"Hah, I wish. When it comes to Kenny, she's got on her rose-colored glasses and I've yet to convince her she really needs to take them off. I try to see it from her point of view. She finally decided to give another man a break, to trust Kenny—for my sake. And now she just can't bear to admit she got it wrong again."

"I guess it's understandable," Jace said. "But still. You're her daughter. She should be backing you up."

"Yeah, I wish. You know how I told you I had doubts about Kenny before I caught him with Kimberly?"

"I remember."

"Well, I went to my mom and confided in her. I told her that Kenny wasn't the guy I loved anymore, that sometimes I felt like I didn't even know him, he was so different from who he used to be. She was the one who convinced me my fears were groundless, that I only had a very normal case of pre-wedding jitters, that Kenny was a wonderful man and it was all going to be fine."

Jace touched her hair again, gently, an easing kind of touch. "So your judgment about the guy was solid. And your mom couldn't—and still can't—let herself see the truth. I'm betting she'll get the picture in time."

"I hope so."

"And the main thing is that you didn't go through with it. You had the guts to turn and walk away. You're a strong woman. And you're going to be fine."

Joss could have stayed in Jace's arms all night. But she'd had her head on his shoulder for several minutes now—too long really. She needed to pull herself together, no matter how good it felt to lean on him.

She sat up and retreated to her end of the sofa. That time, he didn't try to stop her, and she was glad that he didn't. If she was going to have a man for a friend—even just for a week—it was nice to think he was the kind of guy who would know when to put his arm around her.

And when to let her go.

"Mostly," she said, "I think I'm doing pretty well, you know?"

He gave her a slow nod, his dark eyes steady on hers.

"I tell myself I'm getting past what happened last Saturday. But every time my mom calls, she just brings the whole mess into painful focus all over again. Her blindness to the reality of the situation makes me see way too clearly what a huge mistake I made." She held up her thumb and forefinger, with just a sliver of space between them. "I got this close to marrying a guy who cheated on me on our wedding day—and with my own cousin, no less."

"But you *didn't* marry him. Focus on that, Joss."

She braced her elbow on the sofa arm and rested her chin on her hand. "You're right, I didn't. But I did quit my job for that rotten, no-good cheater. I gave up my cute apartment. When I go home, I'll be starting all over again."

"Maybe you can get your job back."

"Maybe I can. We'll see." She straightened her spine. What she wanted right now was a long bath accompanied by an equally long, totally self-indulgent crying jag. "Thank you for listening—and I need to stop whining."

He gave her a slightly crooked smile. "I have the strangest feeling you're giving me the boot." He picked up his beer from the coffee table and downed the last of it.

"It's only, well, lately talking to my mom really brings me down." She tried to think of something snappy and charming to say, so they could end the evening on a happier note. But right then, she was all out of snappy, totally bereft of charming.

He rose. "It's the great thing about a best friend. Even a best friend for a week. You don't have to explain anything. All you have to say is good night."

Jace thought about Joss all the way out to Jackson and Laila's place.

He hoped she was okay. And he hoped he'd done the right thing by leaving when she asked him to.

What else could he have done? She'd had that look. Like all she wanted was to get into bed—alone—and pull the covers up over head. He'd figured the best thing he could do for her right then was to get lost.

Jackson and Laila had ten beautiful, wooded acres with a big two-story farmhouse, a barn and a paddock where they kept a few horses. When Jace pulled up in front of the house, the lights were off upstairs. But through the shut blinds of the front room's picture window, Jace could make out the faint glow of the flatscreen TV. He figured he would find his brother in there, channel-surfing, waiting up.

Jace was right.

Jackson sat in his favorite recliner, the mutt he and Laila had adopted from the animal shelter snoozing at his feet. Jace entered the room and Jackson turned off the TV. "Beer?"

"No, thanks." Jace dropped into the other recliner and popped out the footrest. "Good party at the Rib Shack."

Jackson grunted. "Ethan get after you?"

"Yeah."

"He thinks he's going to talk you into coming in with us."

"It's not gonna happen."

"Yeah." Jackson set the remote on the table by his chair. "I told him that. More than once. But you know how he can be when he gets an idea in his head."

Jace closed his eyes. He felt comfortable. Easy. It was always like that with him and Jackson. Even when they fought—which they used to do a lot when they were younger—there was a certain understanding between them. They didn't need a lot of words. They just accepted each other.

The mutt's collar jangled as he scratched himself. The dog's name was Einstein. He wasn't much to look at, but Jackson claimed he was really smart.

Jackson said, "You know, I thought you said you'd sworn off women. But you're in Thunder Canyon barely twenty-four hours and already you've got a girl."

"No, I don't." Jace gave the denial in an easy tone, knowing his brother wouldn't believe him.

"Shame on you, Jason. Lying to your own twin brother."

"Joss is great. I liked her the first minute I saw her. But it's not like that. We're just friends."

Jackson chuckled. "Yeah, and if you think I believe that, I've got some oceanfront property in Kansas to sell you."

"I mean it. We're friends. She's here for another week. I'll be hanging around with her if she'll put up with me, but nothing's going to happen between us."

"Hey, whatever you say. I'm just glad to see you taking an interest in a woman again. And she seems like a great girl to me. Laila liked her, too. So did Ma."

Jace made a low noise that could have meant anything and hid his smile. His family—including his twin—were all so predictable. He showed up with a woman at his side, and they couldn't believe there was nothing but friendship going on.

Which suited him just fine.

Jackson spoke again, gruffly this time. "And it's good, that you came back to Montana finally."

Jace knew he'd hurt his brother's feelings by not coming to Thunder Canyon over the holidays—and worse, he hadn't been there for Jackson and Laila's Valentine's Day wedding.

Time to try and get that behind them. "I'm sorry, Jackson, that I didn't come for the holidays when you invited me. And missing your wedding? That was the worst. I know it was wrong of me not to be there."

Jackson didn't answer for a full sixty seconds at least. Finally, he grunted. "I was pretty miffed at the time—especially that you didn't show to be my best man. But I'm over it."

Jace confessed, "I didn't know my ass from up for a while there. I didn't come at Christmas because of Tricia." He said her name and waited to feel miserable. Instead, he realized, he felt perfectly okay. Apparently, he really was putting all that behind him. "The last thing Tricia said she wanted was to 'head for the sticks over the holidays'—her words, not mine. I didn't even argue with her. I was gone, gone, gone. It was 'Whatever Tricia wants, Tricia gets,' as far as I was concerned. And then it all went to hell. For a couple of months after New Year's, I was operating strictly on autopilot. I went to work and I went home. Then you and Laila decided you wanted a Valentine's Day wedding. I was a mess. I just wasn't up for it."

"Sounds like you're better off without Tricia Lavelle."

"I am. A lot better off. I see that now. But at the time, I was one-hundred-percent certain it was the real thing with her. You know how I've always been. Not a guy who ever gets serious over any woman. So when I actually thought it was love, I went for it. All the way. How wrong could I get? It was a rude awakening when it ended, let me tell you."

"Rough, huh?"

"Bad love will do it to you every time—not that it *was* love. Not that I even have a clue what love is."

Jackson slid him a cautious glance. "The whole family kind of wonders if you're really over her yet."

Jace tried to picture Tricia's face in his mind. Somehow, the image wouldn't quite take form. And then he thought of Joss—her great laugh, how much fun it was just to talk to her, those big brown eyes and all that gorgeous cinnamon-shot coffee-colored hair. He had no trouble picturing his new best friend at all. "Oh, yeah," he told his twin. "I'm over Tricia. I'm ready for a brand-new start."

Jackson chuckled. "Good. You quit your job and you don't want to live in Midland anymore, so it looks to me like a new start is exactly what you're going to get."

Chapter Three

The phone by the bed was ringing.

With a groan of protest, Joss lifted her head from the pillow and squinted at the bedside clock. Nine-fifteen in the morning. Not what you'd call early. Unless you'd lain wide awake until the wee hours, stewing over your bad choices, angry at your mother, wondering what you were going to do with your life....

And the phone was still ringing.

Surely, eventually, it would cycle back to the front desk, because she didn't want to answer it. Who could it be except her mother calling to beg her to come back to Kenny—or Kenny calling to demand she stop being "petty" and quit making such a big deal over a tiny little incident that had meant exactly nothing?

Hah.

She reached over and grabbed the phone and barked into it, "I do not want to hear another word about it. Do you understand?"

The voice of her new best friend answered, "Aunt Melba is going to be disappointed. You know she was really looking forward to seeing you in church."

Joss dragged herself to a sitting position and swiped her tangled hair back off her face. "Ugh. And wait a minute. Did I actually tell her I would be there?"

"No," Jace admitted. "You hedged. Aunt Melba assumed. *I* said you'd be there."

"So thoughtful of you to make my commitments for me."

"Did I mention I brought coffee?"

"Brought? Where *are* you?"

"Waiting in the hallway outside your door."

She grinned. She couldn't stop herself. "That is so not fair."

"Vanilla latte. Just sayin'."

"All right, all right. You sold me." She hung up, grabbed her robe and belted it as she hurried to let him in. When she opened the door, he held out the tall Starbucks cup. She took it, sipped and gestured him inside, shutting the door and then leaning back against it with a sigh. "Yum. Thank you."

"You're welcome." He gave her one of those knock-your-socks-off smiles of his. Really, he was looking great, freshly showered and shaved, in a different pair of expensive boots, tan slacks, a button-down shirt and a nicely cut sport coat.

She grumbled, "At least *someone* got a good night's sleep."

He took in her blenderized hair, the robe, her bare feet—and her grumpy expression. "Sorry to wake you up."

"No, you're not."

"You're right. I'm not." He took her shoulders, turned her around and pointed her toward the bedroom. "Go on.

Get ready. We don't want to be late. Aunt Melba would never forgive us."

"Who's this 'we,' cowboy?" She muttered over her shoulder, but she went. And she took her latte with her.

Twenty minutes later, she emerged feeling church-ready in a pink silk blouse and an oyster-white skirt, with a favorite pair of low-heeled slingbacks in a slightly lighter pink than the blouse. She'd pinned her hair up loosely and worn the pearl earrings her mom had given her when she graduated from high school.

Jace said, "You look amazing."

She realized she felt better. A lot better. Jace seemed to have that effect on her. He cheered her up, had her looking on the bright side, thinking that something exciting and fun could be happening any minute. She grabbed her pink purse and off they went.

Thunder Canyon Community Church, Jace explained, was in what the locals called Old Town, with its narrower, tree-lined streets and buildings that had stood since pioneer times.

Joss loved the church on sight. It was, to her, the perfect little white clapboard church, with tall windows all along the sides and a single spire in front that housed the bell tower. A mature box elder tree shaded the church steps and the small square of front lawn.

The doors into the reception area stood wide as the church bell finished chiming. Inside, the organist was playing something suitably reverent, yet inviting. People smiled and said hello. Melba was there, wearing a blue flowered dress and a little blue hat, standing guard over the open guestbook. She greeted them with an approving smile and showed them where to sign.

Joss signed her name and "Sacramento, California,"

for her address. She felt a little tug of glumness, to be reminded that she didn't have a place to call her own anymore, that all her household possessions were packed up in boxes and stacked in a rented storage unit, waiting for her to figure out what to do with her life.

But the glumness quickly passed when Jace took her arm. They entered the sanctuary and the organ music swelled louder. The sun shone in the tall windows and Jace's brother Ethan signaled them up to a pew near the front. Lizzie, on Ethan's other side, leaned across her husband to greet them as they sat down.

The service was as lovely and comforting as the little white church itself. Joss even knew the words to a couple of the hymns. The pleasant-faced pastor gave a sermon on God's grace, and somehow all of Joss's problems seemed insignificant, workable. Just part of life.

After the service, Lizzie reminded them that she would love to treat them to free muffins at her bakery. Meanwhile, Ethan said he wanted Jace to take a tour of his Thunder Canyon office building.

Jace said, "No, thanks. Gotta go," and herded Joss toward the exit.

Melba was at her post by the guestbook. She told them how glad she was that they had come. "And I want to see you both at the Historical Society Museum very soon. I've been helping out there several times a week. Thunder Canyon is a fascinating place with a rich history. While you're in town, you might as well learn something."

Joss only smiled and nodded. Jace ended up promising he would drop by the museum soon.

From the church, they went over to Lizzie's bakery, where they split a complimentary blueberry muffin and each had a ham and egg croissant and a tall glass of fresh-squeezed orange juice. Jace seemed to know everyone. He introduced her to a guy named Connor McFarlane and his wife, Tori, who was pregnant and just starting to show. Tori taught at the high school. Connor was not only the heir to the McFarlane House hotel chain, but he was also a major investor in the resort.

Joss also met Grant Clifton, his wife, Stephanie, and their little boy, AJ. The child was seventeen months old and adorable, with golden curls and a sunny smile. Stephanie let Joss hold him. He was so sweet and friendly, dimpling at her, laying his plump little hand against her cheek, even leaning his blond head on her shoulder. Joss gave him back to his mom with a little tug of regret. She wished she could have several little ones just like him.

Maybe someday…

Grant Clifton seemed vaguely familiar. When he explained that he managed the resort, Joss realized she'd seen him behind the front desk once and another time at the resort's best restaurant, the Gallatin Room.

That was the great thing about a small town like this one, Joss thought. You could get to know almost everyone. And when you walked down the street, people just naturally smiled and said hi.

After they left the bakery, Jace took her hand. They started strolling west down Main Street, enjoying the sunshine, looking in the windows of the quaint little shops. It felt good to have her hand in his. Really good. Maybe *too* good.

She let him lead her along for another block before she realized they were going the wrong direction and hung back. "Hey, wait a minute. Your car's that way." She pointed over her shoulder. They'd left his fancy SUV back near the church.

"So? It's not going anywhere." He tugged on her hand. "Come on, I want to show you the Hitching Post—you know, that great old bar and restaurant I told you about yesterday?"

She eased her fingers from his grip. "Right, the one where you hooked up with Theresa Duvall."

He stood there on the corner, his dark hair showing glints of bronze in the sun, and looked at her reproachfully. "What did I do?"

She hung her head and stared down at her pretty pink slingbacks. "Not a thing. Sorry, that was low."

"Yeah, it was. But I'll get over it. Hey, look at me."

Reluctantly, she raised her head. His eyes gleamed. With just a look, he made her want to smile at him. But she didn't.

On that corner was a homey-looking restaurant with flowered café curtains in the windows. The restaurant was closed. He stepped into the alcove by the door and tipped his head at her, signaling her to join him.

"We can't stand here on the corner forever," she groused, as an older couple walked past her and went on across the street.

He chuckled. "*We're* not standing on the corner. *You* are." He waved her into the alcove with him. "Come on. Come here…"

Reluctantly, she went. "What?"

He whispered in her ear, "I love the Hitching Post."

"Whoop-de-do." She spun her index finger in the air.

"Joss, about your attitude?"

"Yeah?"

"Lighten up."

She knew he had a point. "Okay, okay. So why do you love the Hitching Post?"

He sat on the wide window ledge next to the door. "Good memories, that's why. When I was a kid, we always used to go there every time we came to town. My dad would take us. We'd get burgers and fries and milkshakes on the restaurant side, where they allowed kids, and it was a special thing, with all of us together, with my dad relaxed and really *with* us, you know, focused on the family? He used to call us his little mavericks. I thought that was so cool. It seems to me that we went to the Hitching Post often, even though I know that we couldn't have. I was only six when he died. And we only got to visit Thunder Canyon now and then in the summer. But I do remember clearly that on our last visit here before he died, my dad took me to the Hitching Post alone, the two of us. For some reason, Jackson didn't even get to come. It was just me and my dad and I was the happiest kid on the planet." He rose from the window ledge. His eyes holding hers, he took a few stray strands of her hair and guided them back behind her ear. A small shiver cascaded through her and she wanted to move even closer to him—at the same time as she knew she ought to step back.

"Okay," she said softly. "I get it now—why that place is so special to you."

"Good." His caressing tone hovered somewhere on the border between gentle and intimate. "I mean, nothing against Theresa, but she's not what I think about when the Hitching Post comes to mind."

Joss felt rotten, and not only for razzing him about Theresa. There was also the uncomfortable fact that she was starting to wonder what it might feel like to kiss him. Plus, she was flat-out envious of him.

He had a great big, terrific family. And he'd had a dad, a *real* dad, until he was six, a dad who hadn't left him willingly. Then, when he lost his dad, he'd gotten kind Pete Wexler as a stepdad. Her dad, on the other hand, had walked out before she even had a chance to know him.

Her family consisted of her and her mom and right now, her mom only lectured her.

He was grinning again. “So come on, let’s go to the Hitching Post.”

“I don’t know. It’s past noon. Maybe I should just go back up to the resort.”

His grin faded. He blew out a breath. “Okay, Joss. what’s up with you?”

“I just…I feel low now, that’s all.”

“Why? A few minutes ago you seemed to be having a great time.”

“I was.”

“So what happened? You realized you were having too much fun?”

She opened her mouth to tell him how off-base he was, but then she saw that he might actually have a point. “I keep thinking I can’t just hang around in Montana doing nothing forever.”

“You’re right, but there’s no problem. You’re only hanging around in Montana doing nothing for another week. Then you can go back home and knock yourself out finding another job and a new apartment.”

Now she felt hurt. Really, her emotions were all over the map today. “How can you make a joke of it, Jace? It’s not a joke.”

“I know it’s not.” He said the words gently. And then he asked, “Are you bored?”

“No!” She wasn’t. Not in the least. “Are you kidding? I’m having a great time—or I was, just like you said, until a few minutes ago. And then, I don’t know, all at once I felt low and cranky.”

Jace stuffed his hands in his pockets. And then he just stood there next to the glass-topped, café-curtained door of the closed restaurant, watching her, waiting.

She busted herself. “Okay, my life’s a mess. And right now, I feel guilty about it. I mean, at least up at the resort I’m busy being defiant, you know? Having my un-honeymoon, hating all men. But here, with you…” She didn’t know quite how to explain it.

Jace did it for her. “Here, with me, you’re having a good time. And you don’t feel you have the right to have a good time. And not only are you having a good time when you don’t have the right to, but you’re also having it with a *man*.” He widened his eyes and spoke in a spooky half whisper. “A man you just met…yesterday.” She didn’t know whether to laugh or punch him in the arm. Then he put on a look of pretend disapproval. “Face it, Joss. Your mother would never approve.”

“This is not about my mother.” She said it with way too much heat. “And I really, well, I just want to go back to the resort now. Please.”

He gave her a long look. And then he nodded. “All right, but would you do one little favor for me first?”

She resisted the sudden need to tap her foot. “Fine. What?”

“The Town Square’s back there about two blocks. It’s that small park we passed after we left the bakery?”

“I remember it. What about it?”

“We’ll stop there, sit on a bench under a tree and talk a little bit more. And then I’ll take you back up Thunder Mountain.”

She folded her arms across her middle and looked at him sideways. “Talk about what?”

“I don’t know. The weather, the Dallas Cowboys, the meaning of life…”

“Oh, very funny.”

“We’ll just talk, that’s all, about whatever subject pops

into our heads. And not for long, I promise. Half an hour, max. Then it's back to the resort for you."

She accused, "I know you're going to try and make me feel better about everything. Don't deny it."

"I wouldn't dream of denying it. Yes, Jocelyn Marie, the ugly truth is I am going to try and make you feel better. That is my evil plan. So what do you say? The Town Square? A measly little half hour of your time?"

He didn't wait for her answer, but only reached for her hand again.

The little park was a lovely, grassy, tree-shaded place. They found a bench under a willow, the drooping branches like a veil, hiding them from the rest of the world.

"Nice, huh?" he asked her, after brushing a few leaves off the bench seat and gallantly gesturing for her to sit first. She did, smoothing her skirt under her, crossing her legs and folding her hands around her knee. He dropped down next to her. "Kind of private. If we whisper, no one will even know we're here."

She laughed. He really was so charming. "How *old* are you, ten?"

"Only at heart. Tell me a secret."

She gave him a deadpan stare. "You first."

He thought it over, shrugged. "Once I kissed a toad."

"Eeww. Why?"

"Jackson dared me. He was always a troublemaker. And I was his second banana, you know? He would come up with these wild-ass ideas and I felt honor-bound to go along. But then, somehow, if there was something gross involved, he would always manage to get me to go first. Then he would mock me. Once I kissed the toad, he told me I was going to get warts on my lips."

"Oh, that's just mean."

"He could be, yeah. But he's also…the best, you know?"

"How?"

"He'd take a bullet for me. For anyone in the family. That's how he is. You can count on him. Even in the old days, when you never knew what stunt he was going to pull next, you always knew he had your back."

"So you're saying he's settled down, then—from the days when he made you kiss that toad?"

Jace nodded. "He was the bad boy of the family. He drank too much and he chased women and he swore that no female was ever going to hogtie him. But then he met Laila. She changed his tune right quick. Now he's got a ring on his finger and contentment in his heart. I've never seen him as happy as he is now." He studied her face. His gaze was warm. She thought how she was kind of glad he'd insisted they come here before he took her back up the mountain, how being with him really did lift her spirits. "Your turn," he said. "Cough up that secret."

"I always wanted to get married," she heard herself say. "Ever since I was little. I wanted…a real family. I wanted the family I never had. A man I could love and trust. Several kids. Growing up, it was always so quiet at home, with just my mom and me. My mom likes things tidy. I learned early to clean up after myself. So our small house was neat and orderly, with a hushed kind of feeling about it. I dreamed of one of those big, old Craftsman-style houses, with the pillars in front and the wide, deep front porch—you know the kind?"

"I do."

"I dreamed of bikes on their sides on the front lawn, of toys all over the living room floor, of spilled milk and crayon drawings scrawled in bright colors on the walls, because the children who lived there were rambunctious and adventurous and couldn't resist a whole wall to color on. I dreamed of a bunch of laughing, crying, screaming, chattering kids, everybody talking over everybody else, of music on the stereo and the TV on too loud. And I saw myself in the middle of all of it, loving every minute of it. Me, *the Mom*. And I saw my husband coming in the door and stepping over the scattered toys to take me in his arms after a hard day's work. I pictured him kissing me, a real, hot, toe-curling kiss, the kind that would make our older kids groan and tell us to get a room."

"Wow," he said. "That's a lot better secret than kissing a toad."

A leaf drifted down into her lap. She brushed it away and confessed, "I always felt guilty about my dream for my life, you know? My mom did the best she could. But all I wanted was to grow up and get out of there, to find my steady, patient, good-natured guy and start having a whole bunch of rowdy kids."

"Joss." He touched her hair again, so lightly, guiding a hank of it back over her shoulder. "I'm beginning to think there is altogether too much guilt going on in your head."

"Yeah, probably. But my mom tried so hard, she *worked* so hard, to do right by me, to make a good life for me."

"Just because you dreamed of a different way to be a mom doesn't make your mom's way bad."

She gave a low chuckle. "You amaze me, you know that?"

"In a good way, I hope."

"In a great way. When I met you I thought you were just another hot guy trying to get laid. But instead, you're a shrink and a philosopher, with a little Mahatma Gandhi thrown in for good measure."

He arched one of those thick, dark eyebrows. "Just don't tell Jackson, okay? Not the part about Mahatma Gandhi anyway. He would never let me live it down."

She uncrossed her legs, folded her hands tightly in her lap and stared miserably down at them. "I have another secret. A bad one."

He teased, "*Really* bad?"

"Yeah, really stinkin' bad. I'm beyond embarrassed to admit it."

He didn't say anything. He just waited, not pushing her.

So she told him. "For the first two days I was here, staying at the resort, I was fully planning to work things out with Kenny, take him back and marry him anyway, in spite of what he did with Kimberly in the coat room." She paused, waiting for him to say how he couldn't believe she would ever give a jerk like that another chance.

But he only sat there, waiting, his expression unreadable, giving her a chance to tell him the rest.

So, grimly, she continued. "Within an hour after I ran from the church, I was already thinking of how I was only going to make Kenny suffer for a while, make him grovel at my feet and beg me to give him another chance. And then, once he'd admitted what a complete jackass he'd been, once he'd sworn never to do anything like that again, I would take him back. I was thinking that he could give me that big Craftsman house I wanted. I was thinking that with him, I could afford to have all those kids. I was thinking that I had chosen him and been with him for five whole years because he was the one to help me live my dream. I told myself all that, even though long before the wedding day, I already knew very well that he wasn't the sweet guy he used to be, that he'd changed, become a smug jerk I didn't even like being around. But still, I had bought my mom's pep talk and gone ahead with the wedding anyway. Because I'm almost thirty and if I didn't settle for Kenny, I might never find anyone better." Deeply ashamed, Joss fell silent.

Jace was silent, too, sitting there beside her on the bench under the drooping branches of the willow tree. Somewhere in the little park, she heard children laughing.

A child called, "Mama!"

And a mother answered, "Right here!"

"Watch me swing high!" the child commanded.

"I'm here. I'm watching...."

Jace asked, "So what changed your mind?"

She'd come this far. She might as well admit the rest. "Kenny failed to grovel. He called six times those first two days. And every time he called, it was only to say the things he said yesterday—you know, in the Lounge, when you overheard me talking to him? He self-righteously explained to me that *I* was being unreasonable, that *I* had completely humiliated *him*, that *I* had it all wrong. That there was nothing between him and Kimberly and I ought to realize there wasn't and quit acting like *I'm* the one who got messed over." She crossed her legs again. "By the end of the second day, I finally had to admit that there was no salvaging things with Kenny, that it was Over, capital *O*, and I was going to need to make myself a whole new life."

"So...would you take him back now, if he wised up and was honestly sorry for cheating on you, if he got down on his knees and swore you were the only woman for him? If he promised he would never even look at another woman again, that he would do anything—*anything*—for one more chance with you?"

She didn't even have to think about it. "No way. I'm through with him. Done. That ship has sailed. It's as Over as Over gets."

He stood. "Well, all right, then." He held down his hand to her.

She stared at those long, tanned fingers of his, puzzled. "What?"

"I'll take you back to the resort now."

A certain wistfulness curled through her. She tipped her head back to look up at him. "Now you want to get rid of me. You're disappointed in me."

"Hell, no. I think you're terrific. You were with that guy for years. Makes sense it took time to accept that it wasn't going to work out. And in the end, you made the only workable decision about him—after giving him a chance to come clean and make things right. There is nothing to be disappointed about in that. But I did promise you that after we talked for a while, I would take you back up the mountain." He still held out his hand.

She took it. Really, she could get used to holding Jace's hand. He tucked her fingers over his arm and led the way out from under the willow tree, across the grass to Main Street, where they turned back the way they'd come, toward the car.

Twenty minutes later, he pulled into the turnaround beneath the porte cochere at the side of the resort's clubhouse. A valet stepped up to open the door for her. She waved him off and turned to Jace behind the wheel. "I have to ask, did you study psychiatry in school?"

He grunted. "Are you kidding? Petroleum engineering, with a minor in business."

Softly, she told him, "Thank you—for keeping after me until I told you what was bothering me. For listening."

"Hey, what's a best friend for?"

"I had a really good time. At that beautiful little church, at the bakery. Even sitting under that willow tree telling you things you don't even need to know. That part wasn't fun exactly. But it was very…therapeutic, I guess you could say."

He nodded. "Happy to help."

She was suddenly absolutely certain he only wanted to

get rid of her now. And why wouldn't he? She had totally blown it with her sulking and feeling sorry for herself, with her icky revelations about how she'd actually thought she might marry Kenny anyway, even if he was a cheating SOB, because he had money and could give her the life that she wanted. Her throat felt tight. She coughed to loosen it. "Ahem. Well, I'll…see you later, then."

"Later."

She hooked her pink bag on her shoulder, pushed on the door and the valet appeared again to open it all the way for her. "Uh, thanks," she said, and got out. The valet gave her a friendly smile and shut the passenger door. Joss stood there, feeling forlorn, as Jace drove away.

His Range Rover had disappeared from sight when the awful realization hit her like a smack in the face. His family was "in oil." He drove an eighty-thousand-dollar car. The price of a pair of his fancy boots would have paid the rent on her lost apartment for a couple of months at least. True, like her, he was between jobs. But Joss Bennings being out of a job and Jason Traub quitting the oil business were two completely different things.

Jason Traub was a rich guy. A very rich guy. She would bet her whole savings account on that—her significantly reduced savings account. There had been a lot more a year ago, before she'd paid for the wedding and the reception that hadn't happened after all. But even if she hadn't spent all that money on her nonwedding, her total savings still wouldn't be more than chump change to someone like Jace. She knew he had to have an inheritance and a nice, fat stock portfolio. He didn't really *have* to work.

And now that she'd told him the truth about her goals, what could he think but that she was trolling for a good provider so she could buy a big house and raise a bunch of boisterous kids? He must be wondering if she'd set out to get her hooks in him. He'd probably decided that she'd been giving him an act, pretending to hate men when she was really looking for a guy with big bucks to replace the no-good cheater she'd left at the altar.

Joss let out a small moan of misery. She *liked* Jace. A lot. She really did want to be his friend. She *loved* being his friend. And she'd been looking forward to spending more time with him before she went back to Sacramento and got to work picking up the pieces of her life.

But now she'd gone and ruined it with him. She just knew that she had. She tipped her head back and let out another moan.

"Ma'am?" asked the valet, looking worried.

She pulled herself together, pasted on a smile and shook her head. "I'm okay. Really."

Another vehicle rolled under the porte cochere and the valet stepped forward to open the passenger door. With a heavy sigh, Joss turned for the glass doors that led into the clubhouse.

Chapter Four

In her suite, Joss tossed her purse on the table in the foyer and went straight to the bedroom, where she shucked off her shoes and fell backward across the bed. As she stared blindly at the peaked ceiling, she tried to make up her mind whether to call Jace and swear to him she wasn't after him in any way, shape or form—or if the wiser course would be to leave bad enough alone.

And then she realized she didn't even have his number, so the question of whether to call didn't matter anyway.

The phone on the nightstand rang. Joss told herself not to answer it. The last thing she needed right now was another lecture from her mother or more crap from Kenny.

But then, as always, she couldn't stand to let it ring. She reached over, picked it up and put it to her ear. "What now?"

"You're my best friend for the whole week and I don't have your cell number. How wrong is that?"

"Jace." She breathed his name like a grateful prayer. Tears blurred her eyes and clutched at the back of her throat. "Hey."

A silence on his end, then gruffly, "Are you all right? Did something…happen?"

She blinked, swallowed, let out a slow breath. And told him the truth. "I was sure that I'd totally freaked you out. That you had to be thinking I'm some kind of gold digger."

He made a bewildered sound. "Whoa. Wait. *Why*?"

"Okay, now I hear your voice, it all seems completely ridiculous that I could have thought that."

"Joss, why?"

"Because of what I told you. About marrying Kenny anyway, even though he cheated and I caught him in the act, marrying him because he had money and could, um, support me in the style to which I hope to become accustomed."

"Oh, right." He was smiling. She could hear it in his voice. "The big, messy house and all those loud, undisciplined kids who really shouldn't be allowed to color on the walls."

"You can get special paint, you know. Washable paint. And yeah, that would be it—the style to which I can't wait to become accustomed."

"Listen to me, Joss. Are you listening?"

"Yes."

"I don't think you're a gold digger. Not in any way. Got that?"

"Yeah."

"So can I have your cell number?"

She rattled it off. "And can I have yours?"

"Absolutely." He gave it to her. She rolled over and scribbled it down on the complimentary notepad by the phone. "And about tonight," he said, "dinner at Jackson and Laila's? I'll pick you up at five-thirty."

She grinned to herself. She'd never actually told him she would go, but so what? She *wanted* to go, and she was going to go.

"I'll be waiting," she promised. "Outside, under the porte cochere, where you dropped me off just now."

Jackson's house was wall-to-wall family and friends.

To Jace, it looked like just about every Traub in the state of Montana was there, not to mention all the Traubs from Texas. And there were other well-known Thunder Canyon families represented. There were Cateses and Cliftons and Pritchets, all of them related to the Traubs—if not by blood or marriage, then by the bonds of longtime friendships.

Friends and family filled the big living room, the kitchen and spilled out onto the wide front porch and into the tree-shaded backyard. Jackson had a professional-sized smoker barbecue going along with an open grill. The mouthwatering aromas of mesquite-smoked ribs, barbecued chicken and grilling burgers filled the air.

Jace had arrived with Joss just a half hour ago. She was a knockout in dressy jeans that hugged every curve and a silky shirt the color of a ripe plum. He'd whistled at her when she got into the car at the resort. Hey, even a best friend could show his appreciation when a woman was looking good.

His plan had been to keep her close at his side all evening, so his mother wouldn't have a chance to start working on her, pumping her for information about "how things were going" between them, trying to convince Joss that she would love living in Midland, Texas. But within fifteen minutes of their arrival at Jackson's, Laila had dragged Joss off to look at some old picture albums. He'd tried to stick with them, but Jackson had called him outside to help him flip burgers.

And now Ethan had caught up with him. "We need to talk. Come with me," Ethan commanded.

Jace shouldn't have followed, but he knew he was going to have to face his big brother down at some point. Might as well get it over with. Ethan led Jace to the edge of the yard, to a secluded spot beneath a cottonwood tree, where he commenced to put on the pressure.

"I just want you to drop in at the office for a few hours tomorrow," Ethan coaxed. TOI Montana had its offices on State Street not far from the Town Square. "Let me show you around. You can see how far we've come in the past year." Ethan had made the move to Montana only the summer before. "The shale oil operations are surpassing even my expectations."

"I know you're doing a great job, Ethan. I've seen the reports, but tomorrow's a busy day. Remember? We're all taking off in the morning, going riding up Thunder Mountain for that family picnic."

"That's right." Ethan frowned. "I forgot about the damn picnic. Tuesday, then—or come in early tomorrow. The ride up there doesn't get under way until ten or so. We won't have a lot of time, but at least I can show you the corner office that has your name on it."

Jace thought how he'd be happy to admire the new offices. But if he did, Ethan would only be all the more certain that he could talk Jace into coming back to TOI. "I'm out of the oil business, Ethan. I know I've told you that more than once."

Ethan blinked. "Aw, now, Jace. You know you don't mean it. You're an oilman to the core."

"I *was* an oilman. Not anymore."

Ethan reached out and hooked his arm around Jace's

neck, getting him in a headlock, then fisting his free hand to scrub a noogie on Jace's head—like he was five again or something. "Snap out of it, little maverick," Ethan muttered, using the pet name their father used to use on them. "What else you plan to do with your time? We Traubs might have more money than we know what to do with, but that's because we're hard workers. We earned every cent and we *keep* earning until they lay us in the ground."

"Let me loose, Ethan." Jace said the words quietly, but he'd had about enough.

Ethan let go. "I didn't mean to get you all riled up."

Jace ran a hand back over his hair. "Oh, right. Put me in a headlock and pull a noogie on me and then say you didn't mean it."

"I'm only trying to help you get your head on straight."

"It's my head. And it feels plenty straight to me."

Ethan gentled his tone. "All I'm asking is for you to come and have a look at what we've built here."

"And I would be more than happy to do that, if that was all you were up to."

Ethan's lip curled, and not in a smile. "You calling me a liar, kid?"

Jason really wanted to pop his big brother a good one, but he valiantly managed to keep his fists at his sides. "In case you've forgotten," he said way too softly, "I'm thirty-three years old. I haven't been a kid for a long time now."

"Well, stop acting like one, then. Ever since you tangled with Jack Lavelle's little girl, you've been moping around, throwing your life away, acting like you don't care about anything anymore."

Again, Jace reminded himself to hold his temper. "Ethan, you don't know what you're talking about."

"The hell I don't."

"You're here in Montana. And I've been in Texas. And

Ma and Pete have been filling your head full of their own assumptions about what's been going on."

Ethan demanded, "So what *was* going on?"

"Nothing the least mysterious. I want to find a different kind of work, that's all."

"And Tricia Lavelle didn't break your heart?"

"It's a long story. I don't want to go into it."

"Hah. She did a number on you. You're the last single maverick in the family and it's getting to you."

"Will you stop it with the maverick talk? I'm not six anymore. And Ethan, you're not Dad."

"You fell for Tricia, thought you'd finally found your woman. But she dumped you flat, crushed your hopes and walked all over your tender heart. Admit it."

"I'm not admitting anything. Get off my back."

But Ethan just kept on. "You *love* the oil business. You always did. You love it the most of all of us in the family—next to me, I mean."

"People change."

"I don't believe that," Ethan insisted. "Not for a minute. You got your heart broken and that set you on a downward spiral and all I'm trying to do is help pull you out of it."

"Look, Ethan, how many times do I have to tell you? You've got it all wrong. You've been listening to Ma and Pete. And they don't know what they're talking about."

"They know you were going to marry Tricia Lavelle. And then suddenly, it was over. And you were dragging around like someone shot your favorite hound dog, saying how you were through with the oil industry and getting out of Texas."

"It's not their business. And it's not yours either. Give it up."

"I'm only explaining that I get the picture, loud and

clear. You're a mess, Jason, and what you need is to come back to work."

"I have *been* at work. Until last Wednesday, as a matter of fact. I have remained at work well past the time I was supposed to be finished because Ma and Pete pulled every trick in the book to get me to stay. But I'm done now. And I am not going back."

"A man needs to work."

"And I plan to work. Just not for TOI."

"Then doing what, Jason?"

"Something completely different. A business of my own, something hands-on."

"TOI is hands-on. It's *our* company."

"Listen, Ethan, I don't know another way to say it. I'm done at TOI and I don't know yet what I'll be doing next."

"You don't know yet," Ethan echoed in a smarmy sing-song. "Well, that's okay, because *I* know. You're coming to work for *me*, here, in Thunder Canyon."

They were head to head by then, and Jace knew exactly where this discussion was headed. Nowhere. As always, Ethan thought he knew it all. And Jace was not about to be bullied into going back to work doing what he *didn't* want to do anymore. "Back off," he said. "I mean it. Let it go."

"You're my brother. And I love you. And I'll bust your fool head open before I let you ruin your life."

Jace's fists burned to start flying. But what would hitting Ethan prove except that, along with all his other shortcomings, he couldn't control his damn temper even stone-cold sober? They were grown men, for pity's sake. Well beyond the age of imagining they could settle a problem with a brawl. There was nothing more to say here. He turned to walk away.

Apparently, Ethan got the message at last. He spoke wearily to Jace's back. "Aw, come on, Jace..."

Jason wanted to keep walking, but what good was that going to do either of them? Ethan could be a pushy, overbearing SOB, yes. But his heart was in the right place. Jace made himself face his older brother again.

Ethan said ruefully, "You know I only want to help."

"Well, you're *not* helping."

Ethan threw up both hands. "I only thought…a little tough love, you know?" He shook his head. "Lizzie warned me to stay out of it. You have no idea how much I hate it when she's right."

Jason almost grinned. "Why? Because she's right most of the time?"

"She's one hell of a woman, my wife. But she's too damn smart."

"You know you wouldn't have it any other way." His brother's mention of Lizzie had Jace thinking of Joss. He really had to go and find her before Ma did. He said, "The truth is, I'd been thinking about making some changes for a while now—since before I met Tricia, as a matter of fact."

"I…didn't realize that."

"Well, now you know. Ma and Pete hate to see me go. They're going to be on their own in Midland and even though they still want to run the show there, they don't like it that all of us have pulled up stakes and moved on."

"Yeah," Ethan said gruffly, "I get that. They didn't like it much when I left either."

"Whatever they've been saying, I really have changed my mind about the family business. I want another line of work. Something completely different. No, I haven't figured out what yet, but I'm not coming back to TOI. And I really need to go find Joss now."

One side of Ethan's mouth quirked up. "You thinkin' Ma's gotten hold of her?"

"I seriously hope not. Gotta go." He scanned the yard

as he headed for the back door. No sign of a hot brunette in snug jeans and a purple shirt. And no sign of his mother either.

He went up the back steps and into the kitchen. "Do you know where I can find Joss?" he asked Laila, who was arranging the food buffet-style in the breakfast nook on a long, wide table covered with a red-and-white striped tablecloth, decorated with flags and red, white and blue candles and sparkly little red, white and blue Uncle Sam hats.

Laila flashed him her dazzling beauty-queen smile. "Did I tell you I really like her? She's fun and down-to-earth."

"Yes, she is."

"And she loved looking at the pictures of all you Traubs as little kids. She told me she appreciated getting to see some of the old photos of your dad—Charles, I mean. She said you have his killer smile."

"I'll bet she did," he muttered drily. "But where is she now?"

"You know, I think I saw her in the dining room a few minutes ago. She was chatting with your mom."

Jace stifled a groan. "Thanks." He made a beeline for the formal dining room. No sign of Joss in there—or of Ma either. He moved on to the living room.

And spotted them right away, sitting on the sofa, their heads bent close together. His mother was saying something. Joss was laughing and nodding. She didn't look the least overwhelmed. Whatever Ma was filling her head with, apparently it wasn't all that scary.

But still. Joss was kind of jumpy about men—and for good reason. He didn't need his mother freaking her out with too many personal questions and a boatload of assumptions about what was really going on between the two of them.

He headed over there to rescue her.

His mother saw him coming. She gave him a big, wide smile. Joss turned to meet his eyes. He breathed a sigh of relief to see she looked completely at ease.

Maybe Ma was minding her own business after all.

But then he got close enough for her to speak to him. "Jason," his mother said, suddenly looking way too innocent. "Ethan really needs to talk to you. He's been looking all over for you."

"He found me." Jace tried not to scowl. "We had a nice, long talk. I think I cleared up a few...misconceptions for him."

"Oh?" Claudia gave him the arched eyebrow. "What misconceptions do you mean?"

"Long story, Ma. But the upshot is, Ethan understands now that I'm not going to stay in Midland and I'm not going to work at TOI anymore—not in Texas, and not here in Montana."

His mother shot Joss a nervous glance. "Jason, really. This is neither the time nor the place to go into all that."

Oh, right. Now things weren't going the way she'd planned, suddenly it was better if they didn't talk about it now. *Way to go, Ma.*

And he had to give Joss credit. She simply sat there looking gorgeous and completely unconcerned about whatever antagonistic undercurrents might be churning between him and the woman who'd given him life.

He said cheerfully, "Just clueing you in, Ma." And then he bent and kissed her still-smooth cheek.

She grabbed his arm and held him close enough that he could smell the light perfume she always wore. Softly, she told him, "I love you very much. You know that."

"I know. And I love you, too, Ma." He rose to his height

again and spoke to Joss. “Hungry? The food’s on.” He held down his hand.

She took it and rose to stand beside him and he felt like a million bucks suddenly, just holding her slim, smooth fingers in his. “Great getting a chance to visit with you, Claudia,” she said.

His mother was all smiles. “I’m so glad we were able to talk a little. And don’t forget we would love to have you ride up Thunder Mountain with us tomorrow. The picnic will be such fun, and the views from up near the tree line are stunning.”

“Thank you for inviting me,” Joss said. “But…didn’t you mention that you’re riding *horses* up there?”

“Yes, we are. It’s a beautiful ride.”

“I’ve never ridden a horse in my life.”

“First time for everything,” Ma said brightly. “And there are always calm, even-tempered horses available from the resort stables, mounts they keep especially for beginners.”

“I’ll, um, talk it over with Jace.”

“Wonderful.” His mother beamed.

He asked, “You coming to eat, Ma?”

“I think I’ll find Pete first.”

“Well, all right, then.” He guided Joss ahead of him. She led the way toward the kitchen. After a few steps he caught up with her and spoke low so only she could hear. “So are you moving to Midland?”

She laughed, a soft, enticing sound. “It was suggested.”

They entered the dining room. He pulled her over to a quiet corner where they could talk for a moment or two undisturbed. “What else was ‘suggested’?”

“Your mother said she thinks I’m lovely—her word—and she’s so glad you and I met and she really has a wonderful feeling about me.”

“Well, three things Ma and I can agree on at least.”

"Hey, at least *your* mom knows she's meddling."

"Don't be too sure about that."

"But I *am* sure. She wants you back in Texas, but she knows she's out of line to keep after you. She gets that you're all grown up and that it's your life."

"She said all that?"

"Well, not exactly. But I can see it in her eyes."

"Why am I not reassured?"

"You should be. You should take my word for it. Backing Claudia off is going to be a piece of cake—unlike someone *else's* mother I could mention."

Jace wasn't so sure. "Ma filled Ethan's ears with a whole bunch of complete crap about me. He decided he had to come to my rescue with a domineering attitude and some 'tough love.'"

"Yikes. Just now, you mean?"

He nodded, admiring the pretty arch of her eyebrows, the juicy curve of her mouth. She really was easy on the eyes. He'd never had a best friend so good to look at—but then, all his other friends were male and looking at them didn't do a thing for him.

She said, "I hope it all worked out."

"It did. I only *wanted* to punch his lights out."

The brown eyes widened. "But you kept your cool."

"Yes, I did, surprisingly enough. Ethan and I are on the same page now. And I have to agree that siccing Ethan on me was probably Ma's main move. That didn't work, so she'll be about out of ways to get me to come to my senses and get back into life as I've always lived it. But don't kid yourself. She's not finished working on *you*."

Joss tugged on the collar of his shirt. He leaned down even closer. Her warm, sweet breath teased his ear as she whispered, "If she knew the truth about me she might actually believe that we really are just friends."

He whispered back, "Are you saying you're planning on telling her the truth?"

She held his gaze. "Are you?"

"I *have* told the truth, that you and I are just friends. Is it my fault that no one will believe me?"

"I guess not."

"I'm glad you see it that way." Leaning close to her, breathing in the tempting scent of her perfume, it would be so easy to wish for more than friendship. "As for *your* truth, well, it's not mine to tell."

She smiled up at him then, causing his heart to beat harder in his chest. "I appreciate that, Jace. Because I don't want to go into it with everyone. It's too embarrassing."

"That's A-okay with me. I won't say a word."

"Thanks." Now those big brown eyes looked at him trustingly. He felt minimally guilty about that. After all, he did find her way hot. And if she just happened to decide she wanted some benefits in this temporary friendship after all, well, every moment he was with her, it got harder to remember why a few benefits wouldn't be a crackerjack idea. "For some weird reason, I don't have any trouble telling *you* all my secrets—even the shameful ones." Her cheeks flushed pink and she lowered her gaze so she was looking at the second button of his shirt.

He couldn't resist using a finger to tip her chin back up. He stared at her mouth. How could he help it? She had the softest, widest mouth he'd ever seen. He wanted to kiss her. A lot. But he wouldn't. He said, "There's nothing shameful in wanting your dream so much you're willing to compromise to get it."

"That depends on the compromise. Even letting myself *imagine* I might get back with Kenny after he betrayed me with my own cousin…uh-uh. *That* was shameful."

"Listen to me, Joss. I want you to stop beating yourself up about that."

"It's only…"

He put a finger against those soft lips of hers. "Take it from your new best friend. It's over with the cheater. You *didn't* go back to him. That's what matters." From the corner of his eye, he saw everyone filing past, moving toward the kitchen. His brother Corey and his wife, Erin, glanced their way. Erin whispered to Corey. He could just guess what she was saying—something about how Jace had found someone special.

Which was great. It fit into his plan just fine.

He and Joss would have a good time together, enjoying each other's company, taking each day as it came. And his family would leave him alone to pursue what they all hoped was the beginning of a "meaningful" relationship, a relationship that would help him get over Tricia, whom they were all so damn certain had broken his heart.

"Everyone's heading for the kitchen," Joss whispered. "Shouldn't we join them?"

He draped an arm around her slim shoulders. "Let's go."

Chapter Five

"No way. I'm not going anywhere on a horse," Joss informed Jason for what seemed like the hundredth time that evening.

By then, they were back up at the resort in her suite, eating chocolate from the complimentary bowl on the coffee table. She added in a tone she intended to be final, "I'll just take a pass on the family picnic, if you don't mind."

"But I do mind." He put on a needy expression. The guy had no shame when it came to getting his way. "You'll break my heart if you don't go."

She had the bowl in her lap. She fished around in it and found what she wanted. Swiftly, she unwrapped the tempting square of lovely, smooth bittersweet perfection. A groan of pleasure escaped her as she popped it into her mouth. It was fabulous. Too fabulous. Shiny wrappers littered the coffee table in front of them. "Your heart," she said, "is way too easy to break."

Now he looked noble—in a soft-eyed, far-too-appealing way. "It's true. Please. Don't hurt me any more than I've already been hurt. Come to the picnic with me tomorrow. Save me from my family. I'm begging you, Joss."

"So how exactly have you already been hurt?" She *was* kind of curious about that woman who had apparently dumped him.

He actually stuck out his lower lip. "It's just too painful to talk about."

"You know you're totally full of it, right?"

He dug in the bowl for another candy. "What? Full of chocolate, you mean?"

She gave him a slow look of great patience. "You're not going to tell me, are you?"

"One of these days…"

"Which day? By my count, we have five days left and I'm outta here."

"Yeah, but we've been best friends for only about twenty-four hours. I need a little more time to…let down my guard."

"Hah." She kept after him. "So, tomorrow, then? You'll tell me tomorrow?"

"Do you really *need* to know?"

"I'm curious, okay?" And growing more so the longer she hung around with him. "Then again, what does it matter if you tell me all about your recent bad romance, or not?"

"So then, you don't *really* need to know."

She gave it up. "No, Jason. I don't need to know."

He beamed. "Great."

She started to root around for another piece of candy—but no. She really didn't need another piece of candy. Resolutely, she handed him the bowl. "Don't let me near that again tonight."

"Count on me to save you from yourself—and come to the picnic tomorrow."

"Do you *ever* give up?"

"No, I don't. It's not in my nature." He dug in the bowl and pulled out a nutty caramel chew. "Damn, these are good."

"You had to remind me." She reached for the bowl.

He jerked it away. "Uh-uh. Remember? You're not having any more."

"Just one."

"You won't respect me if I don't hold my ground here." He actually put his hand over the top of the bowl, as if she might try to reach in.

Which was exactly what she'd planned to do. "You can be so annoying. You know that, right?"

"It's for your own good," he said oh so nobly. "You said not to let you."

"Well, I *meant*, don't let me until I *want* you to let me."

He cast those bedroom eyes heavenward. "Women. They have no idea what they want."

"Men. They think they know everything." She scooped up the scattered candy wrappers and started firing them at him.

"Hey, knock that off." He ducked and held up the bowl as a shield.

She fired more wrappers. One got stuck in his hair. "Gimme that candy," she demanded, trying really hard to sound scary.

But he only set the bowl aside—his *other* side—and knocked the wrapper out of his hair. "Sorry. No can do." He deflected with his hands that time.

She was out of wrappers. Laughing, she lunged for the bowl.

He caught her by both wrists before she got there. "Behave," he commanded.

"Let me go." She tried to pull away.

He held on. "Say you'll behave."

"No way."

"Say it. Promise."

"Uh-uh. Forget that."

They were both laughing by then, as she struggled to free her wrists and he held on. She got one hand free and she went for it—reaching across him, grabbing for the bowl.

She made it, too. She shoved her fingers in and came out with a nice, big handful. "Got 'em!" she crowed in triumph, holding her prize high.

"Put those back," he instructed in what could only be called a growl.

"What, these, you mean?" She opened her hand and let them rain down on his head.

He sat very still—for a moment anyway—as the candy bounced off his thick hair and broad shoulders and fell to the sofa cushions and down to the floor. Then, frowning thunderously, he glanced around them. "Look at this mess. Wrappers and candy everywhere."

"It's your own fault. You should have given me the candy when I asked for it."

He let go of her other wrist, but then he only captured both of her arms and made a big show of baring his gorgeous snow-white teeth at her. "You're a brat, Jocelyn Marie. You know that?"

"Yes, I am. And proud of it." She tossed her hair and held her head high.

He leaned in, playfully threatening….

And right then, in the space of an instant, everything changed.

One second, they were tussling like a pair of ill-behaved third graders—and the next second, they weren't. One moment she was laughing and teasing and giving him a hard time—and the next, she wasn't.

Out of nowhere, her breath snagged in her throat. Her pulse spiked and her skin felt sensitized and too hot. All at once, she was acutely aware of his big, warm hands gripping her arms, of his dark, dark eyes and the beautiful, way-too-kissable shape of his lips. Of the scent of him, that was a little spicy and a little green and also electric somehow, the way the air smells right before a thunderstorm.

She watched his eyes—saw them track. From her eyes, to her mouth, back to her eyes again…

She knew what was coming. He was going to kiss her.

And oh, at that moment, she *wanted* him to kiss her.

Wanted to feel his powerful arms banded around her, wanted his breath in her mouth and the rough wet glide of his tongue.

Wanted him to guide her back onto the sofa cushions, to press his big, muscled body so tightly against her, to hold her so close and kiss her so long, and so deep and so thoroughly that she would forget…

Everything.

The mess that was her life. All the ways her plans and her world had gone haywire. All the things she somehow had to fix, to make right, even though she really had no idea how to do that.

She wanted to tear off all her clothes and all of his, too. She wanted to be naked with him, skin-to-skin. Naked with her new best friend who happened to be a man she'd met only the day before.

She wanted forgetfulness. And she wanted it in Jace's big arms.

But then, very softly, he asked, "Joss?" And his eyes were different, clearer somehow, seeking an answer from her.

And she liked him so much then. She liked him more than she wanted the temporary escape his lean, strong, male body offered her.

He was doing the right thing by her. He was giving her the moment she needed.

The choice she needed. The chance to stop now. To say no.

She swallowed, slowly. She pressed her lips together and gave an almost imperceptible shake of her head.

That was all it took.

He let go of her arms and sank back against the cushions. She did the same. Her heart still pounded too hard, her breath came too fast and her body still yearned. But that would pass.

It wasn't going to happen. And that was…good.

Right.

For a long, silent moment, they simply sat there, among the scattered candy and empty wrappers, not looking at each other.

And then, without a word, by a sort of tacit agreement, they both rose and began gathering up the pieces of chocolate. She went and got the wastebasket by the wet bar and they threw the wrappers away.

Finally, he started to turn for the door, but then he stopped and faced her, where she stood by the sofa, still holding the wastebasket, feeling forlorn.

"Tomorrow," he said. "You're coming. Don't argue. Wear old jeans and bring a jacket. Tennis shoes if you don't have riding boots. Do you have a hat?"

Gladness surged through her. Suddenly, she desperately wanted to go. "You'll be sorry. I meant what I said. I do not know how to ride a horse."

"Then it's time you learned." His voice was gentle. Fond. And yet, somehow, an echo of heated excitement seemed to cling to him, to thicken the air between them.

She looked in those dark eyes and she almost wished… but no. It was better this way. Safer. Saner. And lately, she could use all the safety and sanity she could get. She said, "I bought boots and a hat the first day I was here. And a cute Western shirt, too, as a matter of fact."

"I'll be here to get you at nine."

"I think this is a bad idea," she said the next morning when she opened the door to him and he stood there looking one-hundred-percent authentic cowboy in faded jeans and rawhide boots, a worn blue Western shirt with white piping and a blue bandana. He had his hat in his hand.

He gave her a crooked smile that made her feel all warm and fuzzy inside. "You're going to have a great time."

She made a doubtful sound and frowned at his hat. "Is that a real Stetson?"

"Resistol."

She assumed that must be a brand of hat. "Well, all right. Good to know."

He took in her red plaid shirt with its crochet trim and rhinestone studs. "Aren't you the fancy one?"

She tugged on her pant leg, revealing more of her boot. "And don't you love these boots?" They were red, too—beautiful distressed red leather embroidered with hearts and wings and scroll-like flourishes.

"Very stylish."

"As long as I'm going to make a fool of myself, I figure I might as well look good while doing it."

"You look terrific." His eyes said he really meant that.

The memory of that almost-kiss last night seemed to

rise up between them. She felt suddenly shy and looked away. "Thank you."

"Joss," he said gently, "it's going to be fine. Ready?"

"No, but I can't seem to convince you what a bad idea this is, so we might as well get going." She grabbed her jean jacket and her brand-new hat and off they went.

They got to the resort stable before the rest of Jason's family arrived, which was great. She would have a little time to practice riding before they started up the mountain.

The horse the groom led out for her was white with brown spots. Already saddled and wearing a bridle, it seemed somehow a very patient horse. It stood there, flicking its brown tail lazily and making gentle huffing noises as Jace checked the strap that held the saddle on and adjusted the bridle.

Joss stood well away from the animal. "Um, does it have a name?"

"Cupcake," said the groom. He was maybe twenty years old, deeply tanned with freckles and a space between his two front teeth.

Joss cleared her throat. "It's a she, then?"

"Nope. Gelding," the groom answered. So very cowboylike. Never use a whole sentence when a word or two will do.

And okay, now she looked, she could see the, er, residual equipment. "Ah, yes."

Jace thanked the groom. The fellow tipped his sweat-stained hat and ambled back to the stable.

"Come on." Jace held out his hand to her.

She eyed that hand warily. "I don't know. I have a bad feeling about this."

"Come on," Jace insisted. He refused to lower his hand.

So she took it.

He showed her which side to mount from and boosted her into the saddle. Cupcake made a soft chuffing sound but didn't move a muscle. Cautiously, she patted the side of his warm, silky neck. "Okay. Can we be done now?" she asked hopefully.

Jace didn't answer. He adjusted the stirrups. Then he gave her some instructions: how to hold the reins, how to use her legs to help guide the animal. And a bunch of other stuff she immediately filed under the general heading, *Things I'm Too Nervous to Remember.*

He took the reins and led her around in a circle for a while, just so she could get a feel for being on a moving horse. It didn't seem so bad really. Cupcake was a prince. He walked along calmly, never once balking or trying to go his own way.

Within a half hour, she was holding the reins and riding Cupcake in a circle, using her knees the way Jace had showed her. She decided that maybe this wouldn't be so bad after all.

His family started arriving in pickups, some of them towing horse trailers. Jace went off to saddle his own horse and Joss kept practicing, continuing in the circle and also stopping, turning and going the other way. Really, it wasn't so terrible. She was actually getting the hang of it, more or less. On a sweetheart like Cupcake, she might even enjoy herself. When Jason's mom, looking trim and young in snug jeans and a yellow shirt, called out a greeting, Joss raised her hand in a jaunty wave.

At a little after eleven, they were all mounted up and ready to go. They formed a caravan and took the road that led to the resort condos farther up the mountain. But before they reached them, Dax Traub, in the lead, turned off onto a tree-shaded trail.

The rest of them followed. It was nice, Joss thought.

Not bad at all, riding along at a steady pace beneath the dappled shadows of the trees. There was a gentle breeze blowing and the air smelled fresh and piney. She followed directly behind Jace, who rode a big black horse named Major. A proud-looking creature, Major tossed his head and pranced and required a lot more handling than Joss ever could have managed.

She much preferred the calm-natured Cupcake. With him, all she had to do was stay in the saddle and lightly hold the reins. Every now and then, Jace would glance back at her and she would give him a big smile, just to show him that she was doing okay.

Piece of cake. Seriously. She kind of had a knack for this. Who knew? *Jocelyn Marie Bennings, horsewoman.* It had a nice ring to it.

The trail narrowed, but that didn't seem to faze the sure-footed Cupcake. The mountain, closely grown with tall trees, rose steeply to her left. On the right, the drop-off was dizzying, even with all the trees that might help to block a fall. Joss made a point not to look.

Jace called back to her, "You doing okay?"

"Fine. Absolutely. Doing gr—"

She didn't get a chance to finish saying *great*, because Cupcake took his next step and the downward side of the trail crumbled out from beneath his hooves.

Joss let out a strangled shriek and grabbed onto the saddle horn for dear life. She caught one last look at Jace's stunned face and then she and Cupcake were off, heading straight down the mountain, kicking up a cloud of dust in a high-speed, utterly terrifying slide.

Chapter Six

With both hands, Joss clutched the saddle horn for all she was worth. There was a rushing sound in her ears and her heart beat so hard it hurt. She closed her eyes. She closed them really tight.

Why look? She knew she was done for, that poor Cupcake would lose his precarious balance as they skidded down the mountainside. He would topple and roll and she would roll with him—*under* him. Oh, it was definitely not going to be pretty.

The brave horse stumbled. She lost her seat and felt herself starting to go airborne. But somehow, even though her arms felt wrenched from their sockets, she managed to hold on. Her butt hit the saddle again, knocking the wind out of her, sending a sharp crack of pure pain zipping up her tailbone, jangling her spine.

She might have screamed. She wasn't sure. It was all happening way too fast and she was so far from knowing what she ought to do next to try and maybe improve her odds of surviving the next, oh, say, twenty seconds.

At least Cupcake remained upright and she was still in the saddle. So far. She dared to open her eyelids to slits, saw the blur of trees as they flew by, heard the sharp retort of hooves beneath her that told her the brave spotted horse was actually running now instead of sliding, that by some miracle, he had gotten his legs under him and started galloping in a zigzag pattern, sideways and downward, switching back and forth, one way and then the other, weaving between the trunks of the tall trees.

And…was it possible? Were they slowing down a little?

She felt dizzy and realized she'd forgotten to breathe. So she sucked in a quick breath and forced her eyes open wider and wished she hadn't dropped the reins when she first grabbed for the saddle horn. Right now, she didn't dare let go long enough to try to get hold of them again.

Knees. She was supposed to use her knees, wasn't she? Kind of press them together to let Cupcake know that stopping would be really, really good—no. Wait. That was to go faster. She really didn't want to go faster.

She needed the reins, but she didn't have them.

All she had was her voice. She used it. "Whoa," she said, "Whoa, Cupcake." It came out in a croak, but the horse actually seemed to hear her.

Triumph exploded through her as he slowed even more with a low snorting sound. She had her eyes open all the way by then and she could see a sort of flat space up ahead, between two fir trees.

She went for it, letting go of the saddle horn, groping frantically for the reins. And she got them! She tugged on them, saying "Whoa, whoa…"

It worked. It totally worked. Cupcake came to a dead stop right there between those two trees.

Actually, it was a really fast stop. Maybe too fast. And maybe she'd been a little rough with those reins. Cupcake rose on his hind legs and let out one of those angry neighs like the wild, mean horse always makes in the movies.

She really should have grabbed for the saddle horn again.

But before she remembered to do that, she was already sliding—right off the backside of Cupcake.

She landed hard on the same place she'd hit when she bounced high in the saddle that one time Cupcake stumbled. Her poor backside. It would never be the same. She let out a "Whoof!" of surprise as she hit the ground, followed by a low groan of pain.

And then she just flopped all the way down onto her back and stared up at the blue sky between the branches of the two big trees as she waited for the agony to finish singing up and down her spine.

Cupcake, making soft chuffing, snuffling sounds, turned around and stood over her. He nuzzled her temple, snuffling some more.

She groaned again and reached up and patted the side of his spotted head. "Good job," she told him, and then qualified, "basically." Reassured, he backed off a little and started nibbling at the skimpy grass between the trees.

"Joss! My God, Joss!" It was Jason. Judging by the sound of swift hooves approaching, he must have taken off down the mountain after her.

She really ought to sit up and show him that she was okay.

And she would. Very soon. Right now, though, well, her butt really hurt and she didn't have the heart to sit on it yet.

A moment later, she heard him draw to a stop a few feet away. He was off that black horse and kneeling at her side in about half a second flat.

His worried face loomed above her. "Joss…Joss are you…"

"I'm okay," she groaned.

He didn't look convinced. "Can you…move your arms and legs?"

She reached up and touched the side of his face, the same way she had done with Cupcake. "Honestly, I'm fine—well, except for my backside. That could be better."

"I'm so sorry." He looked positively stricken. "I made you come today. I never should have—"

"Shh." She put her fingers against his soft mouth. She really did love his mouth. She almost wished she'd kissed him last night after all, even if it was a bad idea. "It's fine," she said. "*I'm* fine. Cupcake is fine." She laughed a little. "And I have to tell you, *that* was exciting."

He grunted. "Yeah, *too* exciting."

She gave him her hand and he pulled her to a sitting position as she heard more horses approaching.

"She okay?" Ethan asked. Joss glanced over her shoulder and saw Jace's older brother, with Lizzie right behind him.

"Everything works," Joss told them, gathering her legs under her, only moaning a little, as Jace helped her to her feet. "But I'm guessing there will be bruises." She leaned on Jace. He put his arm around her. That was nice. She felt safe and protected, all tucked up close against him.

He said, "There's a doctor available back at the resort. Can you ride back? He can take a look at you."

She put a hand to her head. "My hat…"

"It's halfway between here and the trail," Lizzie said. "We can grab it on the way back up."

Joss stared from Jace to Lizzie and then to Ethan. "I can't believe you guys rode down here on purpose—even to come to my rescue."

Ethan chuckled. “It’s really not that bad.”

“It only seems that way when the trail breaks out from under you,” Lizzie added. “Lucky they gave you a steady-natured mount.”

Joss cast an appreciative glance at Cupcake who continued happily munching the sparse grass. “He’s a champion, all right.”

“Can we cut the chitchat?” Jace insisted, “We’ve got to get you to the doctor.”

She reached back and felt all the places that ached. “Really, it’s just not that bad.”

“Joss, you could have been—”

“Don’t even say it. What matters is I *wasn’t*. Cupcake saved the day and I might end up with a bruise or two and there is no way I’m missing the picnic now I’ve come this far.”

“But you—”

She stuck her index finger in the air. “Wait. Watch.”

“Joss—”

“I mean it. Wait.”

He looked at her like he wanted to strangle her, or at least try to shake a little sense into her. But he did shut up.

She peeled his hand off her shoulder and stepped away from him. “See? Upright and A-okay.” She took a step, then another. It hurt a little. And she bet she was going to be sore the next morning. But she was absolutely certain the damage was only superficial. “Really, I’m okay. See?” She held her arms out to the side. “Ta-da!”

“I don’t like it,” he grumbled.

“Well, too bad. It’s my butt and I say it’s going to be fine.”

Ethan laughed and shared a knowing glance with his wife. “Give it up, Jace. That woman has made up her mind.”

* * *

The trip back up to the trail was nowhere near as thrilling as the ride down. In fact, going upward, it seemed steep, but not scarily so. And they found her hat about midway, as Lizzie had promised.

Jace jumped down and retrieved it for her, scowling up at her as he handed it over. "You *sure* you don't want to see the resort doctor?"

She gave him her widest, most confident smile as she settled her hat back in place on her head. "I am absolutely certain. And tell you what, you don't have to ask again. If I change my mind, I'll let you know."

"What if you have internal injuries?"

"Thank you for getting my hat. And will you please stop worrying?"

"It's only that…" He pressed those fine lips together. "If you end up in a coma, I'll hate myself forever and I'll never forgive you."

"A coma? Maybe you didn't notice. It wasn't my head I landed on."

"You know what I mean."

"Hey, you two! Get a move on," Ethan called from several yards ahead.

Jace just waved a hand at him and kept looking up at Joss, a focused, intense, almost angry kind of look. "If anything happened to you, I couldn't stand it…."

His words warmed her. They…touched her, because he really meant them. He really did care. About her safety, her well-being.

Maybe her life was a mess, but at least she'd found Jason. And he truly was her friend.

"Shh." She bent down to him and she kissed him, softly, quickly, on those perfect lips of his. They felt good, his lips. Even better than she had imagined they might. "Stop worrying," she whispered. "That's an order."

He stared up at her for a moment. He didn't look so angry now. Was that a flash of heat she saw in his dark eyes? But then he frowned. "You're fine? You mean that?"

"I am. Yes."

Shaking his head, he turned and mounted the black horse and they continued upward.

At the trail, the rest of the Traubs were waiting. They congratulated Joss on her excellent handling of a dangerous situation. She laughed and told them that her current good health was all due to Cupcake.

They started moving again, following the narrow, winding trail up the side of Thunder Mountain. It was a gorgeous ride. And Joss appreciated it more fully for having survived the headlong tumble down the cliff. She felt a lot easier on Cupcake, too, a lot more confident that even if she was a complete greenhorn, her horse could handle just about anything that fate might throw his way.

Eventually, they emerged from the trees at a higher elevation, where the wind blew brisk and cool and you could look down and see the lower hills and valleys spread out for miles and miles. From up there, the town of Thunder Canyon looked picture-postcard perfect. She could even see the little white church she and Jace had attended two days before. It really was a beautiful little town.

The Traub women had packed a light meal in their saddlebags. They spread blankets in the sun and enjoyed a leisurely lunch. Joss ate heartily. The headlong race down the side of the mountain had given her an appetite.

Jace stayed close. He seemed to be watching for a sign that she might need a doctor after all. She would glance over and catch him looking at her in that same concerned, attentive way. Every time he did that, she felt all warm and good inside. Protected.

Cared for.

She was starting to see that she really would be okay in the long run. Funny how a near-death experience can snap the world into sharper focus. She was young and smart and strong and she had enough money in her bank account to get by until she found another job.

And hey, after knowing Jace, she had to admit that there were still a few good men left in the world. Not every guy was a cheating jerk.

At three, they were back at the resort stables. Lizzie turned Cupcake over to the groom and felt a little sad to watch him amble away.

Jace said, “I think you like that horse.”

“He’s the best.”

He put his arm around her and she leaned close to him with a sigh. He said, “We can ride again, you know, before the week is out.”

“Yes,” she agreed, and looked up to meet those velvety brown eyes. “Let’s make a point to do that.”

That evening Ethan and Lizzie had the big family cookout at their place. Melba Landry was there. She told both Joss and Jason that she was expecting them at the Historical Society Museum.

“Tomorrow, in fact,” Lizzie’s great-aunt instructed.

Joss had a great time that evening. She helped Lizzie and Rose Traub Anderson in the kitchen. Lizzie was not only a baker but also an excellent all-around cook.

Joss told her about the restaurant she’d managed in Sacramento. “I loved that job,” she said. “I hated to leave it. There was something new happening every night. A little bit glamorous, you know? All the customers dressed for a night out, the snowy tablecloths and the good china, floating candles and an orchid in a cut-crystal bud vase at every table. It was a really nice dinner place, with an excellent wine list and to-die-for desserts. I loved the camaraderie between the front and back of the house. And the chef, Marilyn, was a wonder. Not only super creative with a great reputation, but also the calmest, most even-tempered person I've ever met. People say chefs are temperamental. Not Marilyn Standall. I never once heard her even raise her voice, no matter how crazy things got in the kitchen."

Lizzie asked the next logical question. "Why did you quit?"

Joss almost told her. Lizzie would be easy to confide in, but it would have been a downer to get into all that. So she only shrugged. "Time for a change, I guess. I like running a restaurant, though. Most likely I'll find something similar when I get back to Sacramento."

Later, after most of the Traubs had gone home, Joss and Jason stayed to help bring in the extra chairs from outside and stack the dishes by the sink. Lizzie had a housekeeper who would be in to take care of the rest in the morning.

It was after eleven when they climbed into Jace's Range Rover for the drive back up to the resort.

"Did you have a good time?" he asked.

"The best."

"Mind a little detour?" He started the engine.

She glanced over at him and felt a warm glow move through her. "I'm open. Let's go."

Jace's heart sank as he pulled into the parking lot at the corner where Main Street turned sharply north and became Thunder Canyon Road.

The sodium vapor lamp overhead lit a whole lot of

empty asphalt. And the rustic, shingled two-story building stood dark in the eastern corner of the lot.

He turned off the engine and leaned on the wheel to stare out the windshield in disbelief. "Not possible. Nobody said a word to me…"

"A word about what?" Joss asked.

He gestured at the darkened building. "The Hitching Post. Looks like it's closed."

"Just for the night, right? It's after eleven."

He shook his head. "In the summer, it used to be open Monday through Saturday till two in the morning."

"Maybe they changed their hours? I see a couple of lights on upstairs."

He leaned closer to the windshield until he could see the glow in the second-floor windows. "There are apartments up there…"

She flashed that gorgeous smile at him as she pushed open the passenger door. "Come on. Let's have a look, see what's going on."

They walked across the empty parking lot together, their footsteps echoing in a way that sounded sad and lonesome to his ears. At the sidewalk, they turned for the front of the building, with its wide, wood-pillared porch and the big wooden sign between the windows on the second floor. The block letters were a little faded but still legible in the streetlamp's glow: THE HITCHING POST.

And the long rail was still there, at the sidewalk's edge, the rail that had given the place its name back when it first opened as a bar and grill in the 1950s. To the present day, folks still used that rail to hitch their horses.

Or they used to, at least last summer, when he'd come to town for Corey's wedding.

There was a big white sign tacked to the doors. FOR

SALE, it proclaimed in red letters large enough they were visible even in the shadows of the darkened porch.

Twin signs in the windows that flanked the door proclaimed CLOSED INDEFINITELY in letters as big and red as those on the sign offering the place for sale.

Jace stood on the sidewalk looking at all that darkness, at the sad little glow in one of those upstairs windows. "Closed indefinitely. How is that possible? They did a bang-up business. Everybody in town loved this place. I don't get why it would close. And I can't believe no one even *told* me."

Joss slipped her hand into his and he felt a little better. He was glad for the contact, glad she was there. She said, "You sound like you just lost an old friend."

He turned his gaze to her. There was plenty of light, both from the streetlamp and from the nearly full moon. She'd tipped up her pretty face to him, her big eyes amber-colored right then, and soft with sympathy. Gruffly, he confessed, "I feel like it, too. Damn. I was looking forward to showing you around inside, seeing if that bartender I liked, Carl, was still there. I've been wanting to tell you all about the Shady Lady."

"What shady lady?"

"She was a local legend. Her real name was Lily Divine. She lived in Thunder Canyon back when the town was first settled. They called her the Shady Lady and she owned a saloon by that name, a saloon that stood right here, where the Hitching Post is now. Come on…." He tugged on her hand and she went with him, up the steps, into the shadows of that wide, deserted porch.

She whispered, "Tell me you're not planning a break-in."

He chuckled. "It did cross my mind. But no, I promise. We're not breaking in. I just want a closer look at the For

Sale sign." He read the smaller print at the bottom. The Realtor was Bonnie Drake at Thunder Creek Real Estate. Her name was familiar. Hadn't Ethan mentioned her in the past? Maybe she was the Realtor Ethan had used when he bought the building on State Street for TOI Montana.

Joss asked, "Why? You going to buy yourself a bar and grill?"

"Don't laugh. I just might."

She pulled on his hand until he turned and faced her. "You're kidding."

He busted to it. "Well, yeah. What would I do with a bar and grill?" He joked, "Unless you want to show me how to run one?"

She tipped her dark head to the side, and even through the shadows, he saw the ghost of a smile haunting her way-too-kissable mouth. "It's kind of a nice fantasy. Living in this great little town, running the place where all the locals love to hang out…"

A slight wind ruffled her hair, brought the scent of her perfume to him. She always smelled so good. It occurred to him that if he ever tried again, *really* tried, with a woman, he hoped that maybe she would smell as good as Joss did. Clean and sweet, both at once.

She frowned a little. "What?"

He bent closer, whispered teasingly, "I didn't say anything."

She was studying him. "You had the strangest expression on your face…"

"I was thinking that you smell good, that's all. That I like your perfume."

"Oh." Did her cheeks get pinker? Hard to tell in the darkness, but it seemed that maybe they did. "Well, um, thank you."

"The pleasure is all mine, believe me."

Her eyes seemed so wide right then, and filled with amber light, even in the deep shadows of the dark porch. "Jace?" She sounded slightly breathless.

He encouraged her, "Yeah?"

"You know today, when you came down the hill after me and found me flat on my back?"

"Yeah?"

"I thought how I wished I had kissed you last night." Her words sent a flare of heat moving through him. She added, almost shyly, "I mean life is too short, right? You never know what might happen."

He touched the side of her face. Her skin was so soft. And damn, was she trying to tell him something? "Joss, are you okay? Are you in pain? Do you need to see a doctor?"

She cut him off with a low, sweet laugh. "Stop. I'm fine. That wasn't my point." And then she grew serious again. "It's only, well, in life it always seems like there's plenty of time. But is there really? What if I died and I hadn't even kissed you?"

He gazed down into her upturned face and he never wanted to look away. A moment ago, he'd been kind of depressed, to think that the Hitching Post was closed up, with a For Sale sign on the front door. But suddenly, he didn't feel bad at all anymore. The world seemed full of promise. And hope. Of good things. And every single one of them was shining in Joss's big brown eyes.

"I really don't want you to have any regrets," he said, his voice low, maybe a little rougher than he'd meant it to be.

"But I do have regrets. You know that. About a thousand of them. I've made a lot of mistakes and I—"

"Shh." He touched her sweet lips with his fingers and instructed solemnly, "I want you to let those regrets go."

"I'm working on it."

"And the little problem that we never kissed?"

"Yeah?"

"That's easily fixed."

"You're right," she whispered, tipping that tempting mouth up to him like an offering. "So very easily..."

"We can fix it right now. Here. Tonight."

"Yes." Those bright eyes had a naughty gleam in them. They told him she could be bad—in a very good way. "I think we should."

"Joss..." It wasn't a question. Not this time.

But she answered it anyway. "Yes. Oh, yes."

He lowered his head and tasted her lips for the first time.

Chapter Seven

Joss knew that she shouldn't be kissing Jace.

She was almost thirty, for crying out loud. Old enough to know that nothing messed up a perfectly great friendship as fast as sex could. And what did sex start with?

Kisses.

Kisses like this one. Slow, delicious kisses. Kisses that began so gently, with Jace's wonderful soft mouth just barely brushing hers, with the warmth of his big, lean body so close, but not quite making contact with hers.

Yet.

Kisses that led to touching—oh, yes.

Touching just like Jace was doing right now, his big hands cradling her face, holding her mouth up to him. Wonderful hands he had, strong and slightly callused, and warm.

So warm…

He let them wander.

She knew that he would. She welcomed the slow twin caresses along the sides of her neck as his fingers skimmed downward. Oh, she could easily get used to this, to kissing Jace.

For five whole years, she'd never kissed anyone but Kenny. Really, what had she been thinking?

She'd been missing out, big time.

Jace clasped her shoulders. His lips moved on hers, coaxing. She knew what he wanted.

She wanted it, too. She parted her lips for him and let him inside.

He groaned, a soft, low, pleasured sort of sound. She felt it, too. The beginnings of arousal. Already, her body was kind of melty and heavy in the most lovely, delicious sort of way.

She swayed against him and he gathered her in.

Oh. Yes. Perfect. Her breasts were now pressed against his hard chest. They ached, a little, already. A good, rich, exciting ache. An ache that promised to deepen in the best sense of the word.

His arms were nice and tight around her and she felt cherished and safe and very, very good. And his tongue was doing beautiful things inside her mouth, stroking, exploring. Learning all her secrets—well, a few of them at least.

He lifted his mouth from hers. She made a frantic little sound, not wanting it to end. Not yet.

Oh, please. Not yet….

And then, what do you know? It didn't end. He simply slanted his amazing lips the other way and kissed her some more.

Yes. *This*, she thought in a lovely, foggy, heated wordless way. This was it. *The* kiss. The one she'd known she couldn't afford to miss….

Jace's kiss…

He wrapped her even closer, so tight against him.

Tight enough that she could feel his growing hardness, pressing into her. Her response was immediate. She sighed against his warm lips and pressed herself even closer, lifting her hips to him, eager.

For more.

For sex.

With Jace.

Sex…

Oh, she did want to…

But then what?

The annoying question echoed in her brain, stealing her pleasure in this special moment, reminding her that her life was all upside-down and an affair on the rebound was not a good idea. Her world was way too complicated already. She didn't need to make it more so.

He must have felt her withdrawal. He raised his head and he smiled down at her, so tenderly, his dark eyes low and lazy. "You messed up and started thinking, didn't you?"

"Guilty." She put her hands against his chest. She could feel his heartbeat, strong and steady.

He peered at her more intently. "You okay?"

She nodded. "You are a totally amazing kisser."

And he smiled. "Likewise."

"I would kiss you some more, but…"

"…it's not what we're about," he finished for her. His strong arms fell away and she carefully kept herself from swaying back against him. He offered his arm. She took it. "Come on," he said, "I'll take you back up to the resort."

"Not coming in?" she asked, when he pulled up under the porte cochere.

Jace was thinking he would like to go in. He would like

it a lot, but it seemed too dangerous after that kiss. She'd felt just right in his arms. And the sweet taste of her lips…

That had been something. The way she'd cuddled up close against him had really gotten him going. They might be best friends and not going there. But he had to be realistic. She did it for him. In a big way.

And he needed a little distance. Tonight, he could too easily be tempted to try and put a real move on her. And he got that she wasn't up for anything hot and heavy with him—or with anyone. Not after what she'd been through.

"Not tonight," he whispered. "Breakfast? We can go down to the bakery and maybe—"

"Yes." She smiled an eager smile. And he was glad. They'd shared an amazing, mind-blowing kiss, but it wasn't going to mess things up between them.

The valet opened her door. She got out and then turned back and leaned in to ask, "Nine tomorrow morning? Pick me up right here, under the porte cochere?"

"You got it."

The valet shut the door. Jace watched her turn for the entrance, admiring the easy sway of her hips, entranced by the way all that lush, shiny hair tumbled down her slim back.

During the drive to Jackson and Laila's place, his mind kept circling back to the kiss. To the way she filled his arms, to the feel of her breasts against his chest, to the way she pressed her body to him, lower down, to her soft mouth opening under his…

He thought about kissing her again.

He thought about doing a lot more than just kissing.

The house was dark when he let himself in. He went straight up to the guest room and took a shower. A very cold shower, for a long, long time.

When he got out, his teeth were chattering and his lips

were blue. But the shower had done the trick. He was freezing and sex was the last thing on his mind.

And he'd learned his lesson. He was not kissing Joss again. He was not even *thinking* about kissing Joss again.

Uh-uh. No way....

In the morning before he left to pick up Joss, he joined Jackson and Laila in the kitchen.

"So," he asked his twin, "how long's the Hitching Post been closed?"

"Since March," Jackson said.

"You never a said a word." Jace tried not to sound accusing, but it did kind of bug him that no one had told him. "*Nobody* said anything. Joss and I stopped in there last night and everything was dark."

Jackson sipped his morning coffee and answered with a shrug. "It was a shock when it happened. But you were more or less refusing to communicate at that point."

That was true, Jace had to admit. In March, he'd still been pretty down after the whole mess with Tricia. Half the time, when Jackson or any of his siblings called, he would find some excuse to get off the phone fast, and then not bother calling them back. He hadn't felt like talking to anyone—and he certainly hadn't felt like answering any questions as to what the hell was the matter with him.

"Sorry about that," he said and meant it.

"Hey." Jackson gave him a grin. "You finally seem to be coming out of it. That's what matters."

At the stove, Laila asked, "You want some bacon and eggs, Jace?"

"Thanks, but no. I'm picking Joss up and we're going to the Mountain Bluebell." He asked his brother, "So what's the story? I always thought the Hitching Post was a moneymaker. Why would they suddenly close down?"

"Lance O'Doherty died," Laila said somberly.

Jace blinked. "No." O'Doherty and his wife Kathleen had owned the Hitching Post since it first opened in the 1950s. Kathleen had passed away some years back.

"Yeah," Jackson confirmed. "Lance finally went to meet his maker. The old guy was in his eighties. And he was still going strong right up to the end. Story goes that he went to bed on March first and never woke up on the second. There was no one to take over for him."

"I thought there was a daughter..."

Jackson nodded. "Noreen. She's in her fifties. Plays the harp for some symphony in San Diego. Never married, no kids. Has zero interest in coming back to Thunder Canyon to run her dad's bar and grill. So she shut it down and put it up for sale, cheap. At first, we were all sure that someone would snap it right up. I think I heard that there were a few offers made, but I guess those deals never went through."

Jason shook his head. "The Hitching Post out of business. That's just wrong."

"Someone will buy it eventually," said Laila. "It's been only a few months since it went up for sale. It's a great location, with plenty of parking. I heard a rumor a cousin of the Cateses from Sheridan was thinking about buying the property and turning it into a farm machinery dealership."

"Farm machinery?" Jace swore in disgust.

Jackson chuckled. "People need tractors, Jace."

"And this town needs the Hitching Post."

Jackson sent him a sly look. "Why don't you buy it?"

He thought about last night, him and Joss in the shadows next to the locked-up front door with the For Sale sign on it. He'd teased her that he would buy it and she could teach him how to run it.

But it was only a daydream. A fantasy, like Joss had said.

Laila fished bacon out of the frying pan and onto a

paper towel–covered platter. "Yeah, that would be great if you moved to town. Your brother misses you, you know? We all miss you. Family matters. It matters a lot."

Jackson and Jace shared a look. Jace had missed his twin, too. He only realized how much now he was coming out of the funk that had gripped him for months.

And Thunder Canyon would be a great place to live. Yeah, it got mighty cold in the winters, but he could deal with that. There were still lots of wild, wide open spaces in Montana. He wouldn't mind exploring them. Plus, he'd have the benefit of being near a lot of the people who mattered most to him. And he *was* planning to move.

But he wasn't ready to decide where yet. And as for the Hitching Post…

"I know zip about running a restaurant," he said.

Jackson got up to refill his coffee mug. "No law says you can't learn."

Joss was moving a little stiffly when he picked her up at nine. But she said she was fine.

She laughed. "Hey, you should have seen me when I first got up. It wasn't pretty. But I'm feeling better now that I've been moving around."

And it did seem to him that her stiffness faded as the day went by. After breakfast at Lizzie's bakery, they walked over to the Historical Society Museum on Pine Street. Aunt Melba was there, behind the little desk in the small lobby area of the old building.

"So lovely to see two young, smiling faces," she said. She charged them three dollars each and then gave them a guided tour.

The rooms were small and dark and packed with treasures from the past. There was a whole display dedicated to Lily Divine, the madam who'd owned the Shady Lady

Dance Hall in the 1890s. They learned that some sources claimed Lily hadn't really been a madam at all, but a hard-working laundress who took in women in trouble and helped them to get back on their feet. There was even some dispute as to whether the famous portrait of Lily, nearly nude but for several strategically place scarves, was actually of Lily at all.

Jace couldn't help wondering if that portrait still hung over the bar inside the Hitching Post. He hated to think of someone turning the place into a tractor dealership.

What would happen to the portrait of the Shady Lady then? Would they dismantle the long, gleaming cherry-wood bar that had been built over a century ago?

He decided not to think about it.

Times changed and a man had to learn to roll with the punches. He set his mind to enjoying the time he had left with Joss.

It was going by too fast.

That afternoon, they went riding again. He borrowed Major from Jackson and she rode Cupcake. He took her to a small, crystal-clear lake he knew about on the other side of Thunder Mountain from the resort. It was too cold to swim, but they spread a saddle blanket in the sun and stretched out for a while. She said she was feeling better about her life now, about everything. And she thanked him. She told him she didn't hate all men anymore. And she said that was mostly due to him.

He listened to her talk and drank in her laughter and thought about kissing her.

But he didn't. They were friends. Period. And he intended to remember that.

That night, the family get-together was at Dax and Shandie's. Jace took Joss. They had a great time.

The next day was the Fourth. In Thunder Canyon, that

meant a parade in the morning, a rodeo in the afternoon and a community dance in the town hall at night. He and Joss spent every moment together.

He thought about kissing her a lot that day, especially at the dance. When he held her in his arms, it was all too easy to start remembering how good her lips felt pressed to his.

But he held himself in check somehow. Even though sometimes, in her eyes, he thought he saw an invitation. He had a feeling she wouldn't be entirely averse to another kiss. And when he danced with her, he tried not to read too much into the way her curvy body swayed against him.

That night, he took another long, cold shower before he went to bed. It didn't do a lot of good. His dreams were all about Joss, naked and willing in his arms.

Thursday they played golf up at the resort's golf course. Joss was a really bad golfer.

"I'm worse with a golf club than I am on a horse," she said.

He had to agree. Actually, she had some aptitude for riding. But she was a walking hazard with a golf club. Every time she swung it, turf went flying. The ball, however, rarely budged.

After dinner that night at Corey and Erin's, they returned to the resort and hung out in her suite. He told her he kept thinking about the Hitching Post, that he was actually kind of tempted by the idea of maybe buying the place, of moving to Thunder Canyon and learning how to run a restaurant and bar.

She encouraged him. He was just getting around to hinting that maybe she might consider taking a job managing a restaurant and bar in a great little town like Thunder Canyon when the phone rang.

It was her mother, at it again. He couldn't hear the woman's words, but he could see in Joss's face what she must be saying: Come home to Sacramento and work things out with Kenny. When Joss hung up, her slim shoulders were drooping and all the warm amber light was gone from her eyes. He wanted to take her in his arms and hold her, and promise her that everything would be okay.

But she asked him to leave, said she needed a little time alone. She really was down.

He went back to Jackson's and took another cold shower.

That night he dreamed of Lily Divine—except she had Joss's face. In the dream, he stood at the bar in the Hitching Post and looked up at the painting of the Shady Lady.

And suddenly, the painting came alive. The Shady Lady was Joss, so fine and curvy and mostly naked, lying on her side, braced up on an elbow with her beautiful backside to him, sending him a come-and-get-it look over one bare, dimpled shoulder. He stood there, gulping, hard as a rock.

But then she sat up from the pose she'd been stuck in for more than a century. The scarves that covered her breasts and hips wafted in a warm breeze that had come up out of nowhere—right there in the Hitching Post. She stepped out of the painting and down off the wall, her long hair lifted and coiling seductively around her in that impossible breeze. She reached out her slim, bare arms to him, her eyes gleaming with the promise of untold sensual delights.

And then he woke up.

He lay there in the guest room bed and glared at the darkened ceiling and wondered who he'd been kidding, to think it would be enough for him, to be just friends with a woman like Joss.

She called him at seven Friday morning. "Sorry I was such a downer." Her voice was sweet and husky in his ear.

"Hey," he said a little more gruffly than he meant to, "it's not a problem. You know that."

"I want to go riding one more time before I go...."

Her words hit him like a punch to the solar plexus. *Before I go...*

Their time was ending. Tomorrow was Saturday. And Sunday she was leaving.

A week. It was nothing. Gone in an instant. He'd known that, hadn't he?

So why did it suddenly seem so wrong, so completely unfair, that she would be going, leaving him for good?

He schooled his voice to easiness. "So we'll go riding. Today?"

"Yeah. I thought breakfast first at the Grubstake." That was the coffee shop at the resort. "And then we'd head for the stables. I already asked to have Cupcake ready."

He would need to get the go-ahead from Jackson to take Major again. That should be no problem. "Bring something you can swim in," he said.

"But I thought the mountain lakes were too cold."

"I know a little valley. A wide creek runs through it. It's not so high up and should be warm enough for swimming."

"Sounds wonderful," she agreed.

"The Grubstake, then." His voice was rough again, a little ragged with emotions he didn't even understand. "Give me an hour."

"I'll be there. Waiting."

And she *was* there, just as she'd promised, waiting in the coffee shop, dressed for riding in her red boots and jeans and a blue-and-white checked shirt. They ordered pancake specials, with scrambled eggs and bacon. She was animated and smiling, out from under the cloud of misery that had gotten her down the night before.

"Today and tomorrow," she said, her dark eyes gleaming. “And that’s it.” Did she have to remind him? “I’m going to enjoy every minute of the time we have left.”

Don’t go. The words were there on the tip of his tongue. He shut his mouth over them and swallowed them down.

He tried to remember what a tangled mess the whole thing with Tricia had been, that he didn’t know his ass from up when it came to relationships. That the last thing Joss needed at this point was another man in her life.

A friend, she could handle.

But more?

It wasn’t going to happen. She needed time to get over that asshat Kenny, time to put her life back together, to get on her feet. She didn’t need to get involved with some ex-player ex-oilman from Texas who didn’t know zip about love and was seriously considering relocating to Montana and trying his hand at running a bar and grill.

They finished their pancakes and headed for the stables. By ten-thirty, they were on their way up the mountain. They rode a different series of trails that day, around the mountain, climbing for a time. But then, using a series of switchbacks, heading lower, down into the little valley he’d told her about.

The land belonged to Grant Clifton, the resort’s manager, and his wife, Steph. Last year, when Ethan had invested Traub money in the resort, Grant had been kind enough to issue a general invitation to any Traubs who wanted to swim in the creek there.

“It’s beautiful,” Joss said, when they spread a blanket under a cottonwood at the edge of the creek.

He had a hard time paying a lot of attention to the trees and the clear creek and the rolling, sunlit land. Joss had taken off her jeans, boots and shirt by then. She wore a little black-and-white bikini that looked like polka dots at first glance, but was really tiny white hearts on a black background. She filled it out real nice. He kept thinking about his dream, where she was the Shady Lady and she came down out of the picture and held out her arms to him.

"Jace?" she asked softly. "You okay?"

"Ahem. Fine. Great. Why?"

She laughed then. "Well, your mouth is hanging open."

He shut it. "Is not."

She laughed again and turned and ran to the creek. He watched her pretty, round bottom bouncing away from him and tried not to think about how much he wanted a lot more than he was ever going to have with her. If she had any bruises from her fall the other day, he couldn't see them.

Hugging herself and giggling, she went into the water. "It's cold!" She bent at the knees and got right down into it all the way up to her neck.

"I can hear your teeth chattering," he teased from the bank, admiring the way that thick, long hair of hers fanned out on the water all around her.

"My teeth are chattering because the water is freezing!"

"Don't be a sissy," he taunted.

"You said it would be warm down here in this valley," she accused. "Brrrr."

"It is warm—compared to the lakes higher up."

She rose to her feet, the water sheeting off her body, her hair falling to cling like a lover to her shoulders and the high, proud curves of her breasts. The sight stole the breath clean out of his body and made all the spit dry up in his mouth.

"Well?" she demanded. "Are you coming in?"

He remembered to breathe and he swallowed, hard. "Yes, ma'am." He dropped to the blanket and pulled off his boots and socks. His shirt followed. Then he stood up again to unbuckle his belt. A moment later, he stepped out of his jeans.

Joss gave him a two-finger whistle. "I never saw a cowboy in board shorts before—neon orange, no less." He made a show of flexing his biceps and she laughed some more.

And then he took off toward her at a run. She shrieked as he cannonballed into the water. And when he got his feet under him and stood up, she started madly splashing him.

He dived and grabbed for her legs, yanking them out from under her. Flailing and laughing, she went down, but only for a moment. Then she kicked free of his grip and swam for the far bank.

When he caught up with her, she was trying to climb out on the other side.

He grabbed her shoulders and pulled her back in.

She let out a shriek and went under again.

A moment later, she shot upright. She was quick, he had to give her that. She gave him a shove when he wasn't expecting it. He went down on his back, sending water flying. He heard her laughing as the creek closed over his head.

In a few seconds, he was upright again. They started madly splashing each other, both of them fanning the water for all they were worth, really going to town.

Finally, her hair plastered to her face, water dripping from her nose, she put up both hands. "All right. I surrender. You win. You're the champion."

That made him laugh. "The champion of splashing?"

"Yeah." She swiped a hand over the crown of her head, gathering her hair in one thick swatch, guiding it forward over her shoulder so she could wring the water from the dripping strands. "You don't want to be the champion of splashing?"

He speared his fingers back through his hair. "Depends on the prize."

She made a scoffing sound. "Please. You don't get a prize for splashing the hardest."

He stepped up closer. He couldn't resist. They stood in the shallows by then, not far from the bank and their waiting blanket, with the hobbled horses grazing nearby.

She stared up at him, drops of water caught like diamonds in her long, dark eyelashes, her eyes so bright they blinded him. Damn. She was beautiful. "Jace?"

He couldn't stop staring at her wide, soft mouth. "I want to kiss you."

"Oh, Jace..."

"You'd better tell me not to. You'd better tell me now."

Chapter Eight

She drew in a breath—a sharp little sound. And she argued, “But I don’t want to tell you not to…”

He took her shoulders. Wet. Silky. Cool. Longing speared through him. Sharp. Hot. “Was that a yes?”

“Oh, Jace…”

“Answer the question.”

“Yes.” She said it fervently. Eagerly. “That’s a yes.”

So he kissed her. Kissed her for the second time. Slowly, deeply.

She opened for him and he tasted the sweetness beyond her parted lips. He gathered her close to him, skin to skin, carefully. Tenderly.

The sun was warm on his back and she was so perfect in his arms. He didn’t want to let her go.

But he knew he had to. He lifted his mouth from hers with regret. And he opened his eyes to find hers waiting for him.

She searched his face. “Do you know how much I’ll miss you?”

Don’t go. “Hey, you’re not gone yet.”

She reached up, touched his lips with her cool, smooth fingers. “That’s right. I’m still here. And I’m so glad…” Her eyes shone brighter, wetter. A single tear escaped and trailed down her cheek. He leaned close and kissed that warm wetness away. She whispered, “I’m so glad I met you.”

“Me, too.” He took her hand. “Come on.” He led her up to the bank where he picked up the blanket and moved it out from under the shading branches of the tree.

They lay down side-by-side, faces tipped to the sunlight.

Far off, he heard the cry of a hawk. And then silence, just the rushing whisper of the creek and the wind stirring the cottonwoods.

He closed his eyes. It was one of those moments, so simple. So perfect—him and Joss on a blanket in the sun.

Eventually, they got up and pulled on their jeans, shirts and boots. They ate the jerky he’d brought along in his saddlebag and drank from their canteens. Then they rolled up the blanket and tied it on behind Major’s saddle.

They mounted up and started back the way they had come.

That night, they had dinner with the rest of the family at Rose and Austin’s. Around eleven, they went back to the resort. He stayed until three in the morning. They talked and they laughed. They ate too much chocolate. They watched two movies on pay-per-view: a romantic comedy for her and an old Western for him.

The whole night he kept thinking, *Don’t go, don’t go.* After a while it seemed that the words were there, echoing, in every breath he took, in every beat of his heart.

But he didn’t say them.

And he didn't kiss her again either. Not kissing her was almost as hard as not saying "Don't go." But he managed both somehow. He went back to Jackson's in the early morning hours, had his usual cold shower and climbed under the covers to toss and turn and dream of her.

He was up at daylight. He showered fast and dressed faster and headed for the resort. Luck was with him. He caught Grant in the office complex down the hill from clubhouse and took care of the business that had been nagging at him.

Then he went up the hill, got two coffees at the Starbucks on the first floor of the clubhouse and took the elevator to Joss's suite. He had to knock twice before she finally answered, looking sleepy and tousled and irresistible, barefoot in a cream-colored terrycloth robe.

"I see you brought coffee," she said in a sleepy voice. "Smart man."

Don't go. "Mornin'." He held hers out to her. She took it and sipped, stepping back at the same time so that he could enter. "I have a confession," he said to her back as she led the way into the sitting room.

She paused to send him a look over her shoulder. "Nothing too awful, I hope."

"I'm afraid you're going to be mad at me."

She turned around then, and faced him in the archway to the sitting room. "Better just say it." She sipped from her cup again.

It made him ache all over to look at her, to think that she was leaving, that tomorrow, she would be gone. "I stopped in and saw Grant this morning—you know, the resort manager?"

"I remember Grant."

"I caught him down the hill at his office…"

"Yeah?"

"And I paid your bill."

She had her cup halfway to her lips again, but she lowered it without drinking. Her face had a set look to it suddenly, and her dark gaze was steady on his. "Jace. No."

"Come on. It's not a big deal."

"It's a lot of money. And no." She reached out her hand.

He looked at it. "I guess if you're offering me your hand, at least you're not *too* mad. Right?"

"I'm not mad," she said softly. "I promise." She grabbed his fingers. Heat shot up his arm and he had to stop himself from yanking her close to him and slamming his mouth down on hers. "Come on." She towed him into the sitting room and over to the sofa. "Sit." He sat. She dropped down beside him and set her cup on the coffee table. "I'm…well, I could really get emotional, you know? It means so much that you would want to do that for me."

He set his untouched coffee beside hers. "Just say you're okay with it."

She blew out a hard breath. "But I'm not okay with it. It's not right."

"Sure it is." He tried to look stern and uncompromising. "I can afford it, believe me."

"That's not the issue. I mean, I get why you would want to. I do. And it's so sweet of you, really."

"It's not sweet, believe me," he muttered. "Not sweet in the least. I don't think you get it at all."

"But I do get it. It's about Kenny, right?"

How did she know that? He admitted, "I don't want that lowlife, cheating sonofabitch paying your way here. I just don't."

"Jace." She put her hand on his arm. For the second time that morning, he had to steel himself to keep from grabbing her tight and kissing her senseless. "Listen," she said, "I agree with you. I've been thinking about it, too.

And I've realized that I really can't have Kenny footing the bill. I don't want *anything* from Kenny."

"Good. There's no problem, then. It's paid."

With a low groan, she let go of his forearm. "You're not listening to me. It's not Kenny's bill. And it's not *your* bill. It's mine. And I will pay it."

He almost wished she'd been mad at him, instead of so firm and sure and uncompromising about it. How does a man get through to an uncompromising woman? "Listen. You like me, right?"

Her eyes held reproach. "Of course I do."

"You even trust me. A little."

"I trust you a lot." She almost smiled. "And a week ago, I would have sworn I would never trust a man again."

"So…can't you think of it as a gift from a friend? From your best friend? When you get settled, with a new apartment and a great job, you can feel free to pay me back if it's that important to you. But maybe, over time, you'll see things in a different light. You'll remember that I said I *wanted* to do this. And I meant what I said. I don't want you owing your ex a thing. I want you free of him. And I don't want you spending every cent you've got to *get* free of him."

She gathered her legs up onto the cushions and tucked them to the side. Then she wrapped the fluffy robe closer around her. "It wouldn't be every cent I've got…" She gave a low, sad little chuckle. "Not quite, anyway."

"Let me do this for you, Joss. Please."

"I really shouldn't…"

"Yeah, you should."

She shut her eyes, hung her head. "Thank you," she said, so softly.

He wanted to touch her, but that would be too dangerous. "Glad to do it."

And then she swayed against him, whispering a second time, "Thank you."

What could he do but exactly what he longed to do? He wrapped an arm around her and drew her close. And when she lifted her sweet lips to him, he kissed her, a light kiss, one he didn't allow himself to deepen.

And then he picked up her cup from the coffee table and handed it to her. "Go on. Get dressed. Let's get some breakfast."

Joss wanted that final day with Jace to last forever, but it seemed to fly by even faster than the ones before it.

They went to Lizzie's bakery for breakfast, and then they dropped in at the Historical Society Museum to say hi to Melba. They took a long drive along Thunder Canyon Road, all the way to the steep, rocky canyon for which the town was named.

That night, they had dinner in the resort's best restaurant, the Gallatin Room. They ran into Jace's parents there. Claudia and Pete were still staying at the resort.

Jace muttered resignedly, "I suppose we should go and say hi to them."

"Yes, we absolutely should."

So they stopped by the Wexlers' table for a moment. Claudia said how she and Pete would be there for at least another week. And Joss confessed that tomorrow she was on her way back to Sacramento.

"I hope you'll get Jason to bring you to Midland one of these days very soon," Claudia suggested.

Joss didn't give her an answer, only said how much she'd enjoyed spending time with the Traub family while she'd been in town.

They moved on to their table shortly after that. It was in a secluded corner, so it really felt like it was just the two of them. Jace ordered a nice bottle of wine and the food was wonderful, better than ever, she thought.

Jace thought so, too. He told the waiter.

The waiter said they had a new chef.

"Give him our compliments."

"I'll be more than happy to."

The waiter left, and the new chef came out to chat with them briefly. His name was Shane Roarke. He was ruggedly handsome, with black hair and piercing blue eyes. Joss had the feeling she'd met him somewhere before.

When he left them, Jace gazed after him, narrow-eyed. "I could swear I've met him somewhere before."

Joss nodded. "You know, I was just thinking the same thing…"

He looked at her then, his dark eyes so soft and warm, his mouth hinting at a smile. "Did I tell you that you look beautiful?"

Her chest felt a little tight and a delicious shiver whispered across the surface of her skin. "You did tell me. Twice—three times, counting just now."

"I like that dress."

It was snug, black, short and strapless. "You mentioned that, too."

He scowled. "I hate that you're leaving."

"I know. Me, too."

"But we can't go on like this forever."

She grinned. "You're so right. We've been having way too much fun."

He grunted. "It's got to stop."

She laughed. "Yep." She picked up her glass of wine. "Here's to a new life and a great job—for both of us."

He tapped his glass to hers. "To all your dreams coming true."

* * *

After dinner, he suggested, "We could go into town. I think there's another dance at the town hall tonight."

She shook her head and took his hand. "Let's go up to the suite."

He must have had a sense of what she was up to because something hot and hungry flashed in his eyes. "Maybe that's not such a good idea, Joss."

She knew exactly what he was doing—or trying to do: the right thing. As usual. "Jace…"

"What?" His voice was rough and low.

"It's our last night. I'm leaving in the morning. We may never see each other again."

"Rub it in, why don't you?"

"Come up to the suite with me." She held his gaze. She refused to glance away, to pretend to be shy about this. She wasn't shy. Not with him. With him, she'd always been able to say exactly what was on her mind.

He muttered something under his breath. She thought it was a swear word, but she wasn't sure.

She kept hold of his hand. "Come upstairs with me. Please."

He touched her cheek, smoothed a few strands of hair out of her eyes. "Are you sure? I don't want you to regret anything about the time you've spent with me."

"I'm sure." She searched his face. "But maybe you're not?"

A strangled sound escaped him. "Of course I'm sure. That's not the point."

"I disagree. I think if you're sure and I'm sure, well, what else is there? And don't start in about regrets again. I will never regret spending tonight with you." She whispered, "Could you stand it if I left without making love to you? I know I couldn't."

He actually groaned. And then he lifted her hand and pressed his warm lips to it. "That does it." He breathed the words onto her skin. "Let's go."

In the bedroom of her suite, they stood by her bed, facing each other.

She felt nervous. Apprehensive.

And yet, at the same time, absolutely sure.

The covers were already turned back. There were chocolates on the pillow.

"Your favorite kind," he said. "Dark and bittersweet."

She grabbed up the candy and set it on the nightstand. "I'll never eat them. I'll save them. To remember tonight…"

He grinned at that. Her heart ached. How would she live without seeing that grin of his? "Uh-uh. You should eat them. I'll feed them to you personally."

She turned her head away a little and gave him an oblique glance. "Now?"

"Later." He growled the word.

She swallowed. Hard. "I'm…on the pill, but I should have bought condoms."

He reached in his pocket and brought out four of them. "Okay," he said roughly. "It's like this. I never planned to put a move on you, I promise you…"

She teased, "But you wanted to be ready, just in case I dragged you up here and wouldn't let you go until you made mad, passionate love to me."

"Right." His dark eyes were bright with humor—and heat. "You being such a total animal and all."

She took the condoms from him and set them on the nightstand next to the chocolates. "So, all right, we have chocolate and condoms. We're ready for anything."

He was watching her so steadily. "Joss."

Her heart stopped still inside her chest—and then started in again, swift and hard. "Hmm?"

He took her by the shoulders, his big hands so warm and firm. And then he turned her around, smoothed her hair to the side and over her shoulder out of his way, and took down her zipper in one slow, seamless glide. Her strapless black dress dropped to the floor.

She looked down at it, in a silky black puddle around her ankles. Now, she wore her strapless bra, satin tap shorts, black high-heeled shoes. And nothing else.

He whispered her name again. "I never had a best friend like you before..." And he traced the bumps of her spine, so slowly, with one teasing finger, from the nape of her neck all the way down to where her tap pants rode low on her hips. "Beautiful." The single word was more breath than sound.

She stepped out of the dress and bent to retrieve it. There was a slipper chair a few feet from the nightstand. She tossed the dress on that chair and turned to him.

His eyes were dark fire, burning her in the most arousing way.

She said, "I'm so glad you're here. In this bedroom. With me." And she reached behind her, undid her bra and let it fall away.

He gasped. She found that ragged sound supremely satisfying, not to mention exciting.

"Your turn," she instructed.

He started undressing. He did it really fast, with a ruthless efficiency, dropping first to the side of the bed to tug off his boots and socks, and then rising again to face her as he stripped away everything else, tossing each article away from him as he removed it.

Within seconds, he was naked. He stood before her, so lean and tall and beautiful—yes. Beautiful. Beautiful in the way only a man can be, a beauty of power, of muscle. Of strength.

He reached for her, gathered her to him. She went with a soft, hungry cry.

His mouth came down to settle on hers and his chest was so hot and hard against her bare breasts, his arms so tight around her.

She kissed him. She opened to him. Her heartbeat, so rapid and frantic a moment ago, settled into a lazier, hungrier rhythm.

He took her face between his two hands, kissing her so deeply, so thoroughly, and then he threaded his fingers into her hair, combing the long strands, following them all the way down in one long stroke. He clasped her waist.

And then lower, grasping the twin curves of her bottom and drawing her up and into him—so tight. He kissed her some more. A dizzying, magical kiss. At the same time, he was turning her, guiding her to the bed, still kissing her as he eased her down. She sat on the edge and he bent to her, his mouth and her mouth, fused in a hot tangle of warm breath, of questing tongues....

He came down to her. She opened her thighs so he could kneel between them.

His strong hands caressed her breasts so gently, at first. He learned the shape of them, cradling them tenderly. He teased her nipples into aching hardness.

She swayed toward him, her mouth fused with his, wanting to be closer, aware of the thousand ways he thrilled her, excited her, made her burn. Awash in sheer wonder, she counted those ways: his touch, the taste of his mouth, the rough rasp of his beard shadow against her palms when she caressed the side of his face.

His dear face...

How had that happened? In the space of a week, he had

become so very dear to her. She could no longer imagine her life without him in it.

No. She couldn't.

Not now. Not tonight.

Facing the loss of him would be for tomorrow. In the harsh light of day.

Tonight was for magic. For beauty. For pleasure. For the impossible—her and Jace. Together.

This one time…

For tonight, she could almost be grateful that her world had come crashing down. That her groom had betrayed her. That her dream for her future was shattered. Gone.

She'd lost the life she'd longed for. She was going to have to start over.

But in the middle of her own personal disaster, she'd met Jason. He'd taken her bitterness and transformed it somehow. Made it something so perfect and good and sweet. He'd given her a week she would always remember.

And now, at the end, he presented her with one final gift: tonight.

He broke the kiss, settled back on his knees.

She gave a lost, hungry cry and tried to catch his mouth again.

But he clasped her shoulders, steadying her. She opened her eyes to find his dark gaze waiting. He almost smiled, but he didn't. Not quite.

He let his hands trail down the outsides of her arms, rousing goose bumps of desire, making her sigh.

"Oh, Jace…"

"I dreamed about you…"

She laughed, low, a secret, woman's laugh. "No…"

"Yeah."

"Tell me."

"You were the Shady Lady. It was you in that painting

over the bar at the Hitching Post. Remember, we saw a picture of that painting, that day we went to the museum?"

She nodded. "The Shady Lady, lying on her side, draped in nothing but a few scarves…"

His caresses strayed downward. He clasped her waist, molded the outer curves of her hips, and lower. He laid his warm palms on her thighs. "You do remember, then…"

"I do." She moaned a little. "You're driving me crazy."

"Good. In my dream, you were the Shady Lady and you came out of the picture and down into my arms. The wind was blowing out of nowhere, lifting your hair around your face, and lifting the scarves, too, so they kind of floated in the air around you."

"Wait a minute."

He frowned. "You want me to stop?"

"Don't you dare." She let out a shaky breath. "But…the wind was blowing in the Hitching Post?"

"It was a dream after all."

"Ah."

He cradled her calves, one in either hand, rubbing them a little. "And the wind was warm…."

She was on fire by then, yearning. "Ah. Warm. What happened next?"

He took her left ankle, raised it and slipped off her high-heeled shoe. "I woke up."

She sighed. "Oh, no."

"Yeah."

"Sad…"

"Yeah." He lifted her other foot, removed the other shoe, set it aside with its mate. And then he was stroking her legs again, but this time moving upward, over her shins, her knees, her trembling thighs.

Breath held, she watched him as he eased his clever fingers under the loose, lace-edged hems of her tap pants.

He touched her, both hands meeting at the place where her thighs joined, delving in, parting her.

She gasped as he caressed her, his fingers moving beneath the black satin. He found her, found her sweetest spot without even half trying. And he worked it, making her burn, making her so wet and ready….

Oh, it was heaven. Jace's touch.

She lay back across the bed and let him torment her so perfectly. She moaned out loud; it felt so right. And she lifted her hips to him, sighing, whispering his name, tossing her head, reaching down to clasp his corded forearms, holding on to him as he stroked her, bringing her higher.

Higher and higher…

"Lift up," he muttered low, pulling on the tap pants, guiding them down.

By then, she was wild with desire, lost in her own building excitement. She moaned and she raised her hips and he slipped the tap pants down and away.

And then he leaned closer. And his fingers were touching her, opening her. She knew she was bare to his gaze and somehow, that only fired her need, made her burn hotter.

"Jace. Oh, Jace…"

And then he leaned closer still. She felt his breath, stirring the dark hair that covered her sex.

His breath.

And then…oh, and then…he kissed her. There. Right there, where she was burning for him. He kissed her and he parted her and his tongue slid in to find that sweet spot all over again. His tongue…

How did he do that? He created sensations that were delicious beyond bearing.

She reached down, threaded her fingers in his dark,

thick hair, pulled him even closer. She called out his name, wildly, as he held her in his endless, wet, perfect kiss.

Oh, she was rising, reaching…

And he went on kissing her, his big hands under her hips, tipping her up to him. She didn't want it to end. Not ever.

But of course, the end came. And it was glorious.

With a cry, she hit the crest and went over.

Her body trembled. He held on, drinking from her, doing something impossibly fine with his tongue so that the pleasure expanded, moving out in waves from the core of her, filling her, overflowing, spreading out and out… until it halted, hung suspended on a thread for a world-stopping moment.

And then at last, receding, drawing back, like a shining, perfect wave, retreating to the center of her, where it continued to pulse so sweetly in delicious afterglow.

She lay there, dazed. Wondering.

He eased his hands out from under her hips. He broke that incredible intimate kiss.

And he rose to his feet.

She asked, softly, "Jace?"

He said nothing. She gazed up at him, over his muscled thighs, over the proof of his desire for her, jutting so hard and proud. Over his hard belly and powerful chest.

Beautiful, she thought again. A beautiful man…

Strange. She'd always thought of him as kind. An easy-going, easy-to-know sort of guy.

But he didn't look all that kind right then. And not in the least easygoing.

She saw a roughness, now. A depth of need and emotion she hadn't known in him before. Something that called to the woman in her.

Something undeniably, excitingly, possessively male.

She wanted to reach for him, to beg him to come back to her, but her arms felt so wonderfully heavy, her body limp with satisfaction. Pliant. Slow.

So she simply lay there, watching him, yearning for him, as he turned to the nightstand and took one of the condoms. He had it out of the foil pouch and rolled into place in an instant.

Only then did he come down to her again. She welcomed him, lifting her arms eagerly then, to wrap around his hard, broad shoulders, pulling him close to her, loving the weight of him as he settled on top of her.

He buried his head in the curve of her neck. And he kissed her there, using his tongue, sucking the skin against his teeth. Not hard enough to leave a love bite.

Just hard enough to make her moan.

"Now," she commanded in a ragged, needful whisper. "Please, Jace. Now…"

His hands swept down, along the outer swells of her hips. He guided her legs up to encircle his waist. She hooked her ankles together at the small of his back, and she felt him there, thick and hard and smooth, right exactly where she wanted him.

In one long, sure stroke, he filled her.

She moaned at the wonder of it, and sank her teeth into his shoulder, but gently. Oh, he did feel so good inside her.

He felt exactly right. He filled her so deep.

She wrapped herself closer around him, tightening her grip with her arms and her legs. She rocked against him.

And he answered her, rocking back, finding first a long, sure rhythm, teasing her with it, bringing her fully out of the soft fade of her own satisfaction.

Into renewed pleasure. Into rising again, this time with him, better even than the time before.

Slow and deep and steady…and then faster, harder, faster still.

And she held on, she went where he took her.

Into the heart of the heat and the wonder. Over the moon, into a velvet black night scattered with bursting stars.

Chapter Nine

Later, as they soaked in the suite's jetted bathtub, he fed her the chocolates the maid had left on her pillow.

Leaning back against his broad chest, trapped between his bare, muscular thighs, feeling loose and easy and totally decadent, she let the lovely bittersweet treat melt on her tongue. "I could get used to this."

"Me, too." His voice was a fine, dark rumble in her ear. And along her spine, she could feel the rise and fall of his chest with every breath he took.

She turned her head to him.

He leaned to the side to reach her mouth. And he kissed her. "Um. Chocolate." He offered her a sip of the champagne he'd ordered from room service. She took it, laughing when some of it spilled, those lovely, fizzy bubbles straying down her chin. He said, "I think I'm getting…ideas."

She laughed again. "I feel you." She wiggled back against him. "Oh, my…"

He groaned. “You’ll kill me.”

“With pleasure…” She rolled, floating up, settling against him again, but this time facing him. “What have we here?” she teased, as she found him under the water and wrapped her eager fingers around him.

He made a rough, wordless sound.

She kissed him as she stroked him.

That didn’t last long. A few minutes later, he was gathering her to him, getting his legs under him, rising from the tub, heedless of the water splashing over the sides. He carried her into the bedroom, where he turned so she could reach the nightstand.

She knew what he wanted her to do. Laughing, she grabbed one of the condoms. “We’re dripping water everywhere.”

So he carried her back into the bathroom, where he boosted her up onto the long counter between the double sinks.

“Oh, my,” she said so softly, as he filled her for the second time.

He captured her lips in a long, sweet, wet kiss as he took her over the moon again.

By two in the morning, they had used the last condom. They were back in the bed by then.

She cuddled up close to him and whispered, “I don’t want to go to sleep. I don’t want to waste a moment of the time we have left.”

They spoke of their childhoods. He told her more about his brothers, about the battles between them and also the good times growing up.

She told him about her best friend when she was twelve. “Her name was Jane Ackerman. She dumped me our freshman year to get in with the popular kids.”

"You weren't popular in high school?" He shook his head. "I don't believe it."

"I was shy."

"No way."

"Oh, yeah. And lonely—I told you that the first night I met you."

He answered tenderly. "That's right. I remember."

"I never felt like I fit in, you know? I was something of a misfit, I guess you could say."

"And just look at you now."

She rested her head on his warm, strong chest, where she could hear the steady beating of his generous heart. "You always make me feel so good about myself. Like I could do anything I wanted to do."

"Because you could." His lips brushed her hair.

Her eyelids felt heavy. She let them droop shut. Just for a minute or two…

Joss opened her eyes to sunlight streaming in between the half-drawn curtains.

And to Jason, his strong arms around her, smiling at her sleepily. "Looks like we fell asleep after all."

She snuggled in closer, feeling really good, really relaxed. And really satisfied. "What time is it?"

"Quarter after nine."

"Yikes." She sat straight up and raked her hand back through her tangled hair. "I've got to get moving, get packed. My plane takes off from Bozeman at ten after twelve."

"I'll order room service. You pack. I'll drive you to the airport."

"No need to drive me. I have a rental car."

He looked surprised. "You do?"

She shrugged. "I know. I have taken shameless advantage of you, had you chauffeur me everywhere since that first day we met." She didn't know whether to grab him and hold on for dear life, or burst into tears. "What will I do without you?"

He was braced up on an elbow, looking sleepy and way too sexy. Low and rough, he suggested, "Stay."

Yes! her heart cried.

But then she thought of her mother, of her marriage that hadn't happened, of everything that was so totally up in the air for her. She couldn't run away from her life forever. "Oh, Jace, I wish."

He studied her face for a long, tender moment. And then he said gently, "Well, then you'd better get moving."

She had so much to say to him, but when she opened her mouth, no words came. In the end, she only cleared her throat and answered sheepishly, "Yeah, I guess I'd better." She pushed back the covers. "I'll just grab a quick shower."

"I'll get us some food." He picked up the phone by the bed.

Half an hour later, she was showered and dressed and running back and forth from the closet in the bedroom to the living area, where she had her suitcases spread out on the sofa.

Jace sat at the table by the window, wearing his trousers from the night before and his dress shirt, unbuttoned, in bare feet, putting away a plateful of bacon and eggs. "Come on, Joss. Your food will get cold. Sit down and eat."

She glanced at him, at his beautiful, tanned bare chest between the open sides of his slightly wrinkled shirt. Was there ever a guy as great in every way as Jace? He was smart and fun, thoughtful, kind and generous. Not to mention, superhot and amazing in bed.

Her arms were full of shoes. She wanted to drop them

and run to him, grab him, drag him back to her bed and keep him there all day.

He prompted, "I mean it. Come and eat."

That broke the spell. She couldn't run away from her life anymore. She needed to get back to reality. She was going home to Sacramento today. As planned.

He patted the chair beside him.

She promised, "I will, just a minute," as she dumped the shoes into the biggest of the suitcases and then raced back into the bedroom.

Her wedding gown confronted her. She stopped in the open door of the closet and stared at it, so white, so beautiful— a Cinderella fantasy in the classic ballroom style, with a strapless crisscross bodice sparkling with crystal beading and rhinestones, with endless acres of tulle and glitter net over taffeta that made up the fluffy, cloudlike layers of the skirt.

It was her dream dress.

The one that went with her dream wedding—the wedding she'd run from as fast as she could.

She should just ignore it. Just pack the rest of her things and walk away, leave it hanging there for the maid to find.

But somehow, she couldn't. Somehow, it represented way too much that she hadn't really relinquished. She'd got a great deal on it. But still, it had cost what to her was a small fortune.

She wanted it. She…coveted it. She wanted what it seemed to represent, the life she had planned for herself to which her beautiful, perfect wedding was supposed to be the gateway.

The life she would probably never have after all.

She heard knocking from the other end of the suite. Someone at the door.

Jace called, "I'll get it. It's room service with my extra toast."

She took the dress off the hanger and tossed the bodice over her shoulder, far enough that the acres of skirt were well clear of the floor. Then she took the veil. Cathedral length, it was sprinkled with diamante and edged in lace. She folded it in half and laid it over her other shoulder, so the folded end and the hem end each came almost to the floor in front and in back.

She heard voices in the other room and assumed that Jace was probably overtipping the room service guy.

With one arm wrapped around the dress and the other holding the veil in place, she had all the layers of taffeta and tulle out of the way so that she could see where she was going. She aimed herself at the door to the living area.

She was so busy trying not to trip over all that fluffy fabric that she didn't register Claudia Wexler's voice until she was almost to the sofa and the open suitcases.

"Well, I'm sorry, Jason," she heard his mother say. "I didn't mean to…interrupt."

Joss froze in midstep and glanced toward the arch to the foyer. From where she stood, she could see Jace's back in the open door to the hall and the side of Claudia's face.

Jace said, "Joss is kind of busy, Ma. She's got to get to the airport and she's still trying to pack."

"I only want a word with her."

A word? Oh, Lord. What kind of word? She wasn't up for dealing with Jace's mom. Not right now. Not this morning.

It wasn't even so much that Jace had answered the door barefoot, with his wrinkled shirt wide open, which meant that Claudia had to know he'd spent the night. It was more that Jace's mom would be bound to read more into it than there was—to see it as another proof that Joss and Jace were serious about each other.

And that made Joss feel really bad. Last night had been so beautiful. But look at her now: packing to go. What was she doing with her life? Seriously. Two weeks ago, she'd been about to marry one guy. And last night, she'd done all kinds of naughty, intimate things with another.

Even if he *was* Jace, who just happened to be the greatest guy she'd ever known.

She'd never been the type to go for casual sex.

And last night *hadn't* been casual.

Not exactly.

But it hadn't been the beginning of forever either.

Don't let her see you—or the dress. There was simply no way to explain the dress.

Retreat. Do it now. Joss started to turn.

And Claudia spotted her. "Jocelyn." She craned to the side and put on a too-bright smile. "There you are."

Jace glanced over his shoulder and saw her, too. "Sorry." He mouthed the word.

Joss sucked in a fortifying breath and tried not to think how absurd she must look, buried in a fluffy mountain of taffeta and tulle, frozen in mid-stride just as she was turning to hide. "It's okay, Jace. Really. Claudia, come in."

Now Jace's mom hesitated. Who could blame her? "I honestly didn't mean to butt in."

Jace muttered something under his breath.

His mother glared him. "Well, Jason, I had no idea that you would be here." She aimed her chin high and announced, "Not that there's anything wrong with your being here. You young people have your own ways of doing things. I understand that. I grew up in the seventies. I'm not a complete fuddy-duddy, you know."

Jace stepped aside. "It's all right, Ma," he said resignedly. "Come on in." Looking very uncomfortable, Claudia stepped forward. He asked, "Want some coffee?"

"Oh, no. I won't stay. I have to meet Pete at the Grubstake in ten minutes." Pasting on another smile, she walked past her son and came straight for Joss. "Jocelyn, I only wanted to say—again—that we would love to see you in Midland anytime you care to visit. I have so enjoyed getting to know you. And I'm hoping that even though you're going back to Sacramento, you won't be a stranger. You'll return to see us again and maybe you and Jason…" By then, the fake smile had faded once more. Claudia's voice trailed off. She blinked. "Oh, my goodness." And she stretched out a hesitant hand to lightly brush the frothy skirt of the wedding dress Joss still had draped over her shoulder.

Jace, clearly bewildered at the whole situation, lingered in the arch to the foyer. Joss's frantic gaze skipped from him back to his mother again.

Claudia's face was transfixed. "Is that…" Tears filled her eyes. "Oh, I knew it." She let out a glad cry. And then she was reaching out, grabbing Joss and the Cinderella wedding gown and the endless yards of veil in a hug. "Oh, Jocelyn," Claudia whispered tearfully, her face buried in the dress. "I'm so happy. You two are so right for each other…."

Joss made a sputtering sound. "I, um, well…"

And then Claudia was drawing back, somehow managing to find and clasp Joss by the shoulders, even with the dress and veil in her way. Joss blinked and met the older woman's eyes, which were diamond-bright with happy tears.

"It's a beautiful gown," said Claudia fervently. "Stunning. And I don't really believe in that old superstition that it's bad luck for the groom to see the dress ahead of time. Whatever works, is what I always say. And the two of you…you *work* together. Perfectly. I'm thrilled that you two have realized so quickly how right you are for each other. Jason has been looking for you, Jocelyn—you realize that, don't you? He's been looking for you for much too long now. I think he was giving up hope, if you want to know the sad truth. But now, here you are. Together. In love. Ready to marry and get on with your lives."

"I…uh…" What could she say? How to even begin? *No, see, this is the dress I was going to wear to marry that other guy. As a matter of fact, I've been here on my honeymoon, my* un-*honeymoon. Maybe you noticed I'm in the Honeymoon Suite….*

"Thanks, Ma," Jace said out of nowhere. He sounded sincere. Joss sent him another wild glance. He met her eyes. Held them. And he smiled. The bewildered look was gone. Now he was totally confident. Utterly sure. "We're pretty excited, too."

We are?

This wasn't happening, not really. It wasn't real. Actually, she was still fast asleep in the bed in the other room.

A dream. Yes, it had to be. She wanted to pinch herself, but the dress and the veil and Claudia were all in the way.

Claudia hauled her close and hugged her again. "Have a safe flight to Sacramento. And hurry back. You must come to Midland soon. I can't wait to show you around."

"We're not living in Midland, Ma," Jace said firmly.

We aren't? Joss blinked three times in rapid succession.

He added, "And I'm out of the oil business for good."

Claudia let Joss go and turned to her son. "We'll talk about that."

"No, we won't. There's nothing to talk about. I'm looking into another line of work. And we're staying here in Thunder Canyon."

Claudia sighed. “Oh, Jason…”

“Be happy for us, Ma.” He went to his mother and grabbed her in a hug.

Claudia let out another cry and hugged him back. “Well, all right,” she said in a tear-clogged voice. “All right. If that’s what you really want….”

“It is.” He gave Joss another steady, determined look over his mother’s shoulder. Joss gaped back at him and didn’t say a word. Why speak? None of this was real anyway.

“Then I’m happy for you,” Claudia cried. “I am. So very, very happy.”

“Thanks, Ma.” He stepped back, releasing her.

Still reasonably certain she’d slipped into a dream world, Joss stayed rooted in place, draped in her wedding finery, and went on gaping at the pair of them.

Claudia pulled a tissue from her pocket and dabbed at her eyes. “Oh, I am just so pleased. So very pleased. I can’t want to tell Pete.” With a delicate little sniffle, she asked Joss, “The wedding will be in Sacramento, then?”

“We’re…still in the planning stages,” Jace answered for her.

Claudia waved her tissue. “Of course you are.” She laughed, a teary, soggy, happy sound. “And look at me. Butting in like this. I can see you were trying to enjoy your breakfast.”

“Well, yeah, we were,” Jace confessed.

She stepped close to him again and lifted on tiptoe to kiss his beard-shadowed cheek. “I’ll leave you two alone, then.”

“Thanks, Ma.”

She grabbed his hands. “Just…be happy. That’s all I want for you. All I’ve ever wanted for each of my children.”

“We will,” he answered solemnly. “I promise.”

"That's the spirit." She gave his hands a final squeeze and released them. And then she aimed a jaunty wave at Joss. "See you very soon, dear." She was beaming.

"Ahem. Yes. Bye."

Still beaming, Claudia headed for the door, Jace right behind her.

Joss remained where she was, buried in wedding finery, wondering if she was going to wake up soon.

But then she heard the door click shut and the privacy chain sliding into place.

Jace returned and stood in the arch from the foyer again. "Don't say a word."

She didn't, but she did manage a wild, confused sputtering sound.

He put up hand. "I swear to you, Joss. I have a plan. I think it's a good one. Let me explain."

She found her voice and demanded, still not believing that this could be happening, "A plan? You have…a *plan*?"

"Don't look at me like that. Please. Give me a chance. Hear me out."

About then, she realized she wasn't going to wake up. It wasn't a dream.

Jace had told his mother that they were getting married and moving to Thunder Canyon.

And Joss had just stood there and let it happen.

Chapter Ten

Jace looked into those big amber-brown eyes of hers and knew she wasn't going for it. He felt like a total fool.

But so what? He wasn't giving up yet.

"Come on," he coaxed. "Put the dress down. Eat your breakfast. We'll talk."

She blinked and stared. "I don't have time for talking. I have a plane to catch."

"No, you don't. You don't have to go. You can stay here. With me."

She wrinkled her nose and shook her head in disbelief. "What *planet* are you from? I can't believe that you… I don't… You just…"

He took a step toward her. "Joss…"

"Don't." She lurched away, almost tripping on the veil that hung down her back, but then she stopped. She stared at him, clutching that giant dress, her slim shoulders drooping. And then, out of nowhere she started to cry. "Oh,

Jace." Fat tears trailed down her soft cheeks. "What are we doing? Are we going crazy? What's happening here?"

He felt crappy. Bad. Rotten. And really, for a minute there, he'd thought he'd had a great idea....

And wait. Hold on just a minute. It *was* a great idea. He just needed to convince her of how really perfect it was. "Joss, come on. Don't cry. Please don't cry...." He took another step. She didn't jump away that time, but only stood there, tears dripping from her chin, her nose turning red. "Here," he said gently, "give me all that."

A tiny sob escaped her. "M-my dress, you mean?"

"Yeah. Come on. Give it here...."

She continued to cry, making sad little snuffling sounds, as he eased the big white dress off her shoulder and gently laid it over her suitcases. With a sniffle of pure misery, she asked, "Why did you do that—lie to your mother? It's bad. Very bad. To lie to your mother."

"Give me that, too," he said, and took the giant veil and set it down on top of the dress. He whipped a couple of tissues from the box on the side table and returned to her. "Here, dry your eyes."

She frowned at the tissues, but then she took them. She blew her nose and wiped away the tears. And then she gazed up at him, wearing a shattered expression that somehow managed to be trusting, too. "Now are you going to *talk* to me?"

He took her smooth, slim hand and thought how right it felt in his. She didn't pull away, so he led her to the table and guided her down into the chair in front of her plate. He poured her some coffee, took the warming lid off the plate. "Eat," he said.

She picked up her fork.

And there was another knock at the door.

She stiffened, whimpered, "What now?"

He put his hands on her shoulders, gentling her. "It's nothing. Just the toast I ordered. Eat."

He went to the door, got his toast, tipped the attendant and returned to the living area where Joss was sipping her coffee and staring out the window at the snow-capped peak of Thunder Mountain.

"I'm waiting," she said without looking at him. "This had better be good."

She didn't sound happy, but at least she'd stopped crying.

He set the toast on the table and reclaimed his chair.

She did look at him then. One eyebrow inched toward her hairline. "Well?"

He decided to lay it right out there. "Marry me. We'll buy the Hitching Post. You can teach me how to run it. We'll get a big house with a wide front porch, just like you always dreamed about, on a nice piece of land where we can have a large floppy-eared dog and a couple of horses. And then we'll get to work having a whole bunch of loud, rowdy kids."

She set down her coffee cup and looked at him sideways. "You just want to have sex with me again."

As if he would deny that. "Well, yeah. The sex is great. It's *all* great with us. And come on, think about it. *You* want to get married and have kids. And *I* want you. Here. In Thunder Canyon. With me. And when Ma started in about hearing wedding bells, it all fell into place for me. Why the hell shouldn't we both get what we want? Why should you go? You don't really *want* to go, do you?"

She pressed her lips together and stared out the window again.

He didn't let her off the hook. "Look at me, Joss."

Slowly she turned her head and met his eyes. She wore a

slightly stunned expression. "What?" Her voice was more than a little bit husky.

He rose from his chair. Just enough to capture her beautiful mouth. He kissed her. Hard. "Marry me."

She stared at him for about half a century, dark eyes huge and anxious in her amazing face. Finally, she sighed. "Your mother. I think she really is thrilled at the idea that we're getting married."

"Yeah, so?"

"We just met. Shouldn't she be warning us to take it slow?"

"Joss, she sees what you do for me. She's relieved that I'm back among the living again after months of dragging around like a ghost of myself. She thinks we're good together. Why shouldn't she be happy at the thought that we're making it legal?"

Slowly, she shook her head. "She's just so different from my mom, that's all. If we, um, do this, my mom is going to hit the ceiling. She's going to go right through the roof and it is not going to be pretty. You can take my word on that."

"Don't borrow trouble. We'll deal with your mom together when the time comes."

"But really, our getting married, it seems crazy. Insane. I mean, yeah, you're right about things being good with us. You…do it for me. You're the absolute best. On so many levels."

He felt triumph rising. "And *you* do it for me."

"But get real. It's been a week. It's not like it's undying love or anything."

"So what?"

She kicked him under the table—not hard, but right on the shin.

He winced. "Ow, that hurt."

She had her soft mouth all pinched up. "I don't like you dissing love, Jace. I happen to believe that love matters."

He reached down and rubbed where she'd kicked him. "Okay, it matters. I guess. If you say so. But I mean, well, what *is* it anyway?"

She glared. "What do you mean, what is it?"

"Well, I mean, you loved Kenny Donovan, right?"

She sat completely still for a moment, her face somber, her eyes unhappy. And then, with a heavy sigh, she slumped back in her chair. "I thought I loved Kenny." She shook her head. "Now, though…now, I only wonder *how* I could have thought that. I look back and the only good thing I can say about him is that he seemed like a nice guy. At first."

"Exactly. That's it. *I* thought I loved Tricia Lavelle. And what did I love really? *Who* did I love? I swear I didn't even *know* her. I saw her at a party, standing by a grand piano, wearing a short, sparkly red dress, her long blond hair shining in the light from the chandelier over her head. She looked really good in that dress. And what did I do? Out of nowhere, on the spot, I decided it must be love." He made a low, disbelieving sound. "Me, Jason Traub, in love. I mean, come on. Where did that come from? Until I got a look at Tricia in that red dress, all I ever wanted from any woman was a good time and for her to go away when I was ready to go to sleep."

Joss's expression had relaxed a little. She reminded him, "Your mother said you've been looking for the right woman."

He grunted. "My mother said I've been looking for *you*."

"She meant the right woman."

"Okay. Fine. Yeah. I guess I have been looking lately—for the right woman, for the things that really matter in life, the things I never realized how much I wanted. But love? I meant what I said a minute ago. I honestly don't have a clue about love and I don't even want to go there. I'm just a guy doing the best I can to make my life a good one, to…get involved."

She pulled a face. "Get involved?"

"Yeah. With my…community, you know? With *this* community. Like Aunt Melba said the first day I met her, *'Get involved, young man. Stop sitting on the sidelines of life.'* I admit, I just wanted to get away from her when she said that, but that doesn't mean she wasn't a hundred percent right."

Joss almost smiled. "So." Her velvety gaze sparked with challenge. "The mystery woman's name was Tricia Lavelle, huh?"

He picked up a piece of toast, and then realized he didn't want it after all. He set it down. "That's right."

She put her hand on his arm. It felt good there. He wanted to scoop her up and carry her back to the bedroom. He might keep her there all day and into the night….

But first he had to convince her that they could be a great team in a lifetime kind of way.

"I want to hear about her, about Tricia Lavelle," Joss said, as he'd pretty much expected she would. "I want the story, all of it."

He groaned. "Now?"

She repeated, "All of it."

He pushed his plate away. "It's pretty damn embarrassing. I acted like an idiot."

"Hey, you're talking to the girl who was going to marry Kenny Donovan, remember?"

He held her gaze. "You're no idiot. You always knew what you wanted. And that cheating creep just had you convinced he was it. And from what you've said, he *was* it. At first."

"Thank you." She said it softly. And then she added, "Now, about the thing with you and Tricia..."

Resigned, he explained, "All that happened with her is that I saw a good-looking girl in a red dress and I had a completely out-there reaction. Instead of admitting I wanted what I always wanted—an overnight, totally *un*-meaningful relationship—I decided that I was in love. Which is a complete pile of crap. I'm just not that deep. I have no idea what love really is and I'm better off not kidding myself that I do. I see now that I need to just go for what works and what's right and leave it at that."

She squeezed his arm. "Tell me about her."

"Ack. You're kidding. You want *more*?"

"I do, yes. More."

He tried to bargain. "Tell me first that this isn't going to ruin my chance of getting you to marry me."

She almost smiled, but not quite. "Talk."

So he did. "I met her through her dad, Jack Lavelle. Jack's rich as Rupert Murdoch, a legendary oilman. He was a real-life wildcatter back in the day. In fact, he was once in partnership with *my* dad."

"You don't mean Pete, do you?"

"No, I mean my birth father."

"And Tricia. Is she in the oil business as well?"

"Are you kidding? She might break a nail. Tricia dabbled in modeling. A couple of years ago, she even made the cover of *Sports Illustrated*. But she's never *had* to work. She has trust funds for her trust fund. One look at her in that slinky sequined party dress, standing by the grand piano in the front sitting room of her daddy's Highland Park mansion, all that blond hair falling in golden waves to her perfect ass, singing 'The Yellow Rose of Texas' for her adoring daddy and all his rich guests, and I was gone, gone, gone."

Joss brushed his shoulder with a comforting hand. "It's not so surprising that you fell for her. She sounds pretty fabulous."

"She did *look* fabulous, I'm not denying that. But what's the old saying about all that glitters?"

Joss smiled at him, a rueful sort of smile. "Go on."

"You sure you haven't heard enough?"

"I'm waiting."

"Fine. All right. We spent the holidays in a series of luxury hotels all over the world. For the first time, I thought I understood what it was to be head-over-heels for a woman. I bought an engagement ring with a rock the size of the Alamo. And on New Year's Eve, I went down on my knees and proposed...." He left it there. Maybe she would let it go.

He wished.

"And?" she prompted softly.

"Tricia got cagey."

"Cagey, how?"

"She said she loved me madly, of course. But she was only twenty-four. Much too young to settle down, she said. Couldn't we just go on having fun? And then, in a few years, when she got old—that's exactly how she put it. 'When I get old.' Then we could talk seriously about getting married. She said I could move to Dallas and get work with her daddy. Because Tricia was never, ever leaving her daddy—well, except temporarily, for a prime modeling gig in New York or to lie around slathered with suntan oil, wearing a bikini the size of three postage stamps aboard a friend's yacht on the French Riviera."

Joss said, "And the last thing you ever wanted was to go to work for anybody's daddy...."

He chuckled then, even though he knew the sound didn't have any humor in it. "You got that right. Plus, as I said, Lavelle is in the oil business. And by then I was already thinking I might want *out* of the oil business. I was thinking that I wanted…" He frowned as he let the sentence wander off.

"You wanted what?"

"Truth is, at that point, I didn't really know what I wanted. But it wasn't to spend another five or ten years jetting around the world with some spoiled little rich girl. Suddenly I was seeing my supposedly 'perfect woman' in a whole new—and not very attractive—light. I started wondering what my problem was, wondering what I thought I was up to, generally speaking.

"All the things I'd been sure of in my life—my place in the family business, my no-strings-attached lifestyle—I was all at once itching to change. I'd thought Tricia was the solution to the vague unanswered questions that had started nagging in my brain. But within a few days of her blowing off my marriage proposal, I saw that it was never going to work with her. I realized I didn't even *like* Tricia much."

"So what did you do?"

"I felt so stupid. Here I'd been telling her I would love her forever and now all I wanted was to get free of her. So I tried to be really smooth and subtle. I told her that maybe we ought to cool it for a while."

"What did she say to that?"

"She said that was fine with her. She said that ever since I'd started in on her to marry me, I hadn't been any fun anyway."

"Wow, that was kind of cold."

He grunted. "That was pure Tricia. She's a girl who just wants to have fun—and to live near her daddy."

"So that was the end of it?"

"Yeah. It really bummed me out, you know? But not for the reason my whole family assumes. Not because she ripped out my heart and ate it for breakfast like everyone seems to think. By the end, I didn't give a damn about Tricia—in fact, I'd realized I probably never *had* given a damn about her. I was just glad it was over without any big scenes. But all the questions in my head, about the way my life was going, about my work for Traub Oil, about all of it, those questions were nagging me worse than ever. I realized I had no idea what I wanted. I only knew I *didn't* want the life that I had. I went into a really low period after that."

"A depression, you mean?"

"I don't know if I would call it that. It was just, well, I didn't care about much. I blew off Jackson and Laila's wedding, I was so down. I regret that. A lot. I decided to quit the family business. I had no interest in the things that I used to enjoy."

"Like…casual relationships with women?"

"That's right. Can you believe it? I didn't even care about sex. And before the thing with Tricia, I *always* cared about sex."

She did smile then. "You seemed to enjoy yourself last night."

"Yeah." He drank in the sight of her, those brandy-brown eyes, the lush, delicious curves of her mouth, the thick, cinnamon-kissed waves of her dark hair. "My interest in sex has returned at last. It's a miracle. It started about a week ago. The day I met you."

Her expression turned knowing. "Oh, come on. You told me that day that you only wanted to be friends."

"No, I said I would love to be friends and I accepted the fact that you weren't going to have sex with me. That doesn't mean I wasn't interested. I was. From the first moment I saw you. And that was a great moment for me. It's been six months since it ended with Tricia. And until eight days ago, I had nothin' going on with any woman. No dates, no interest. Not even a spark."

She tried to be cynical. "You're working me, right? To get me to say yes to this wild plan of yours. Next you'll be saying you fell in love with me at first sight."

"No way." He put up a hand, palm out, like a witness swearing an oath. "Uh-uh. I told you already. When it comes to love, I've accepted the hard fact that I have no idea what it is or when I'm in it—that is, *if* I've ever *been* in it, which I seriously doubt. When it comes to love, I'd rather just not go there. The whole subject makes me nervous, you know what I mean? I don't understand it and I prefer just to leave it alone."

She studied his face for several long seconds. "So really, what you're proposing is a practical arrangement."

He knew he was getting to her. He tried not to get too cocky, but he couldn't hide his excitement. "That's right. That's it. You and me—together, a team. Getting everything we want out of life. We…pool our experience and resources. We start a family."

"Wait. *You* want a family, too?"

"Haven't I just been saying that?"

"No. You said *I* wanted a family and you were willing to help me have one."

"Then let me correct that. I *do* want a family. A family with you. Remember when you first told me about your dream for your life?"

"I do, yeah. Sheesh, that was embarrassing."

He didn't follow. "Embarrassing, how?"

"Well, I mean, that even after Kenny betrayed me, I actually considered taking him back…."

"But I told you I could see what you were getting at—that you had a dream, and it was hard to give that dream up."

Her expression softened. "Yeah, you did understand. I really appreciated that."

"And I'm trying to tell you now that when you described your dream to me, I started thinking how great that would be—to be a dad, to be a husband to someone like you, to have a big house with a bunch of kids. I realized something about myself. I was tired of being my family's last single maverick. I knew I could go for just the life you were describing. Seriously, I could. Who knew? But it's true. I think part of what's been eating at me the past several months is I've been wanting what a good-time guy like me never wants and I just wasn't ready to admit that yet. But I'm ready now. I promise you, Joss. I want a great big family. I want that a lot."

Her eyes had that special light in them again. "Oh, this is crazy."

"No, it's not. It's the sanest thing two people can do. To get married because they want the same things out of life, because they're good together in all the right ways."

She picked up her coffee cup, looked into it and then set it back down. "So, if we did this, *when* would we do it?"

"You mean, when would we get married?"

"Yeah." She seemed slightly breathless. "When—I mean, I kind of would like a real wedding, you know? I would like to wear my dress."

He sent a wary glance at the pile of white over on the sofa. "*That* dress?"

She bit her lip. "Tacky, huh? To marry you in the dress I chose to marry Kenny in?"

It did kind of bug him. But come on, what did it matter? It was just a dress. And if she liked it so much, why not? "You want to wear that dress, you wear it."

"Oh, Jace. Are you sure?"

"Absolutely." He stuffed his own discomfort at the thought of her coming down the aisle toward him wearing that dress. "You wear your dress. And we get married right here, at the resort. I'm thinking on the last Saturday of the month."

"*This* month?"

"Yeah. Okay, I know it's quick, but I say we go for it. We put a nice party together for our families and friends in the time we have till then, and after that, we get on with our lives."

Out of nowhere, she jumped up and headed for the bedroom.

He watched her go, too surprised at the suddenness of her leaving to ask her what was up. But then, a few seconds later, she returned with her cell phone. She tapped it a few times. "That's the twenty-eighth? Saturday, the twenty-eighth…"

So, okay. A calendar. She'd brought up the calendar on her phone. She slanted him a sharp look and he realized she wanted confirmation. "Er, sounds about right."

She narrowed her eyes at the screen. "That's twenty days. Tight."

"Joss."

"Um?"

"Is that a yes?"

She glanced up. "Did I mention this is insane?"

"Repeatedly." He pushed back his chair, captured her wrist, took the phone from her hand and set it on the table. "Is that a yes?"

She looked up at him, a little frown etching itself between her smooth brows. "I mean, this would be for real?

This would be a real marriage and we would both give it everything. We would commit ourselves to making it work."

He held her gaze, refused to waver. "That's it. That's the plan."

"You would stick by me always." Tears welled in those fine eyes again.

He knew she was thinking of that bastard Kenny, of how he'd messed around on her. "I would. I swear it. Say yes."

She dashed the tears away. "Oh, Jace…we've known each other only a week. Two weeks ago, I was supposed to be marrying someone else."

"We've been through all that."

"Yes, but—"

"Stop right there."

She blinked. "What?"

"You just said yes. That's the word. Say it again, minus the 'but.'"

"Oh, God, my mother is going to freak."

"Joss, I mean it. Yes or…"

With a little cry, she put her cool, smooth fingers to his lips. "Shh. Wait."

He made a low sound, but he kept quiet. He waited.

And then, at last, she swallowed. Hard. And she nodded. "Yes," she said. "This is so crazy and I can't believe what I'm about to say. But yes, Jace. Yes, yes, yes!"

Chapter Eleven

The moment she finished saying yes, Jace scooped her up and carried her back to the bedroom again.

"You need rest," he insisted.

She laughed at that. She knew that look in his eyes.

And then he started kissing her. She kissed him back, of course. Making love with Jace was a lot more fun than sleeping anyway.

They stayed in bed until eleven or so, which was check-out time. She called the front desk and asked about extending her stay. The clerk said the suite was hers until Thursday. After that, she would have to change rooms.

She hung up the phone and asked, "What now?"

He was still in bed, braced up on an elbow, looking sleepy and sexy and wonderfully manly. "We need to try and reserve a room for the wedding."

So they showered and dressed and went down to the front desk, where the weekend manager was happy to help them out.

As it turned out, the smaller of the resort's two ballrooms was available. They booked it. The manager told them it would be a simple matter to set up the ballroom for the ceremony first, and then bring staff in again to add tables and reset the room for the reception afterward.

That seemed a little complicated to Joss. Would they have to ask everyone to leave and come back later? Jace said they could talk to DJ, maybe see about having the reception at the Rib Shack, if she wouldn't mind the casual atmosphere.

She grinned. "Our first date was at the Rib Shack—sort of, more or less. Remember?"

He laughed. "How could I forget? It was just last week."

"I love that," she said.

"You mean that our first date was only a week ago?"

"No, that our first date was at the Rib Shack, which means it's the perfect place for our reception because it has special meaning for us."

He faked a scared expression. "It makes me nervous when women start talking about special meanings."

She poked him with her elbow. "Get over it—and okay. Speaking more…practically."

He made a big show of looking relieved. "I'm all for 'practically.'"

"Got that, loud and clear. Where was I? Oh, yeah. We can dress up the ballroom really pretty for the ceremony, and then everyone can just go on over to the Rib Shack for the party after."

He agreed. "I'll get with DJ and see what we can do."

They also wanted to arrange for a consultation with Shane Roarke, the Gallatin Room's new chef, to plan a special menu for the reception after the ceremony. Jace said that since the Rib Shack was right there in the resort, it shouldn't be too much of a problem for the Rib Shack and Shane Roarke to work together.

Joss clued him in that top chefs didn't, as a rule, work all that well with others. However, she was willing to go with it, talk to Grant Clifton about the idea. If Grant said it wouldn't be an issue for the resort, then they could approach Roarke about the idea.

They went to the Rib Shack for lunch. And then they made a trip to Bozeman to drop off her rental car at the airport.

Jace insisted on stopping at a jewelry store next. They picked out a ring. It wasn't a hard choice. One look at the one-and-a-half carat marquise-cut solitaire on a platinum band and she gasped. The price brought a second gasp.

Of course, Jace made her try it on, and then decided it was perfect for her. He handed over his credit card and laid claim to the velvet case. The case still held the matching platinum wedding band, which was channel-set with diamonds.

Back in Thunder Canyon, they drove out to Jackson and Laila's house to share the news of their engagement with his twin. As it happened, DJ and his wife Allaire were there. They'd brought their little boy, Alex. Ethan and Lizzie were there too. So was another of Jace's brothers, Corey, and his wife, Erin.

And Laila's single sisters had come. She had three of them—Jasmine, Annabel and Jordyn Leigh. Laila's other sister Abby, who was married to a local carpenter, couldn't make it that day. Neither could her baby brother, Brody.

Everyone was wonderful, Joss thought. They congratulated Jace and really seemed to mean it. They all told Joss that they were so happy to welcome her to the family. The women made a big deal over Joss's ring. She showed it off proudly.

She also spent some time chatting with Laila's sister Annabel, a librarian who owned a therapy dog named Smiley. Annabel and Smiley spent a lot of time at Thunder Canyon General Hospital, working dog therapy magic on emotionally needy patients. Annabel said how great it was to see the last of the Texas Traubs and headed for the altar.

Yeah, okay. Joss felt a little guilty when Annabel said that. Everybody seemed to think that she and Jace had found true love.

But really, what did it matter what everyone else thought? She and Jace had a great thing going. They would have a good life together. A full, rich life, a life they both wanted.

DJ said he'd be honored to host their reception at the Rib Shack. And if Shane Roarke was up for creating a special menu, DJ would see that his staff assisted the chef with whatever he might need from them.

Lizzie insisted that she would bake their wedding cake personally and they agreed to visit her bakery the next day to put in their order. And then Erin launched into a story of how Lizzie had saved the day for Erin and Corey the year before. Ethan's wife had created a fabulous emergency wedding cake at the last minute when the bad-tempered French baker who was supposed to provide the cake skipped town.

Dinnertime approached. Laila insisted they all stay to eat. She had two Sunday roasts slow-cooking outside on the barbecue. There was plenty for everyone.

After dinner, they lingered over coffee and Lizzie's strawberry-rhubarb pie. Joss enjoyed every moment. It was still a little unreal to her that she and Jace were actually getting married at the end of the month. But she could get used to hanging around with Jace's brothers and cousin and their wives. They treated her like one of the family already.

Before they left, Jace went upstairs and packed up his things. From now on, he would be staying with Joss.

He thanked his brother and Laila for their hospitality. Jackson grabbed him in a hug and said again how happy he was for them. She and Jace drove back to the resort in a happy fog of good family feelings.

Kenny called that night.

It was late. Joss and Jace had just finished making slow, delicious love. She'd cuddled up close to him with his warm, hard chest for her pillow and she was fading slowly, contentedly toward sleep.

The phone by the bed rang.

The sound startled her.

Jace wrapped his big arm around her and whispered into her hair. "Don't answer that..."

She kissed his strong, tanned throat. "I have to."

"No, you don't."

"I do. It's ingrained. The phone rings, I answer it."

He chuckled. With some reluctance, he let her go. She reached for it, cutting it off in mid-ring. "Hello?"

"I called your cell twice," Kenny accused. "Aren't you checking your messages?"

She sat up. "Leave me alone, Kenny."

Jace sat up, too. He wasn't smiling. "Can't that jerk take a hint?"

"Who's that?" Kenny demanded. "It sounds like a man's voice."

Jace instructed flatly, "Tell him to get lost." She reached out and silenced him with two fingers against his lips.

He kissed those fingers. "Tell him."

"It is. My God." Kenny was outraged. "There's a guy

with you—in your *room*? Jocelyn, what's happened to you?" He fired more questions at her. "Why is there a man in your room? Why aren't you home? You missed your flight, didn't you?" He heaved an outraged sigh. "This is ridiculous. I've had enough. I thought if I…indulged you a little, you would come to your senses. But this is beyond it. I'm calling my credit card and denying any charges you might incur."

"Go ahead. The bill's already paid."

Kenny sucked wind. "What do you mean paid? I *refuse*, do you hear me? I'm not paying for you to have some strange man in your room. I'll call my credit card company and tell them—"

"I didn't use your credit card."

"What? But—"

"I decided I couldn't stand the idea of taking your money after all."

Kenny made a sputtering sound. Meanwhile, Jace had captured her wrist. He sucked her index finger into his mouth and then ran his tongue around it.

She giggled, mouthed, "Stop that."

He shook his head and sucked some more, using his tongue in a lovely, wet caress. Amazing, really, the things he could do with his mouth. With that tongue…

Kenny demanded, "What is going on with you, Joss? Are you having some kind of breakdown? I don't get it."

She pulled her finger free of Jace's grip—not because it didn't feel really good. It did. But because he made her breathless and she needed all her wits about her to make things perfectly clear to Kenny. "What is going on with me, Kenny, is that I've met someone."

Jace grinned. It was an extraordinarily sexy grin.

"*What*?" Kenny practically shouted.

"I said, I've met someone. He's fabulous. He's asked me to marry him and that is exactly what I'm going to do."

"Joss, you can't. That's completely insane."

Was it? Maybe so. She told herself she didn't care. "Your opinion means exactly nothing to me now, Kenny. I'm getting married the twenty-eighth of this month at five in the afternoon, right here at the Thunder Canyon Resort. As a matter of fact, I'm going to be living here in this beautiful little town with my new husband. We're buying a bar and grill and running it together."

"Wait. No. You're making this up. Just come home. We'll talk. We'll—"

"You're not listening, Kenny. The past couple of years, you never listened. I *am* home. *This* is my home now. I'm never coming back to California, except to get my stuff out of storage and, on occasion, to visit my mother."

"Joss, please—"

"Uh-uh. Forget it. Enough said. Leave me alone. Do not call me again. Goodbye."

"Joss, wait. Don't—"

She hung up the phone. And then she put her hands over her face and let out a groan.

Jace touched her shoulder. "Hey."

She made a vee between her middle and fourth fingers and peeked at him, groaning again. "That was awful. Don't you dare try to cheer me up."

He reached out and pulled her close and settled her head against his shoulder. His beautiful, big body felt so warm and good cradling hers. He even stroked her hair.

She let her hands drop away from her face and allowed herself to lean on him. All of a sudden, she felt totally exhausted. "Ugh. And that reminds me, I should call my mother."

"In the morning."

She let out a short burst of laughter that felt a lot like a sob. "Or maybe never…"

"You just need some sleep," he said. "A little rest and in the morning, you'll feel better about everything."

"What is it with you and all this optimism?"

He chuckled, the sound warm and deep. "It's all going to work out. You'll see."

Was it? Oh, she did hope so. Because seriously, married in twenty days? To this amazing man whom she'd met barely a week ago? Maybe Kenny was right. She'd gone off the deep end—not that she had any intention of backing out of her most recent engagement. No way. If she was crazy, so be it. She wanted to marry Jace.

She sighed. "It's just that we have so much to do."

He captured a swatch of her hair and began slowly wrapping it around his big hand. "Later for all that."

Her mind just kept racing. "And you know, I was thinking that I really need somewhere to stay—we both do, until we find the house want."

"We can stay right here." His voice had gone husky. She knew that dark, hot look in his eyes.

And in spite of her anxious thoughts, a little spark of excitement bloomed low in her midsection. She tipped her head back, kissed his manly square jaw, and insisted, "No way can we stay here."

"Why not?"

"Because it's ridiculously expensive. Plus, the suite is booked starting next Thursday, remember?"

He unwrapped her hair from around his hand only to raise the strands to his face and rub his cheek against them. "So we'll get another suite."

"Jace." She pulled away enough to catch his dear face between her palms. "It's almost three more weeks till the wedding. And it could be months before we find our place. Months at these rates? Forget about it."

He kissed the tip of her nose. "You're worth it."

She lifted up to lightly bite his ear and whisper, "I like the way you say that, but come on, there has to be another option."

He made a low, growly sort of sound. "I'll see what I can do, okay? But now, you should kiss me."

She caught his earlobe between her teeth again and teased it with her tongue. "I know what you're planning...."

"Kiss me."

She blew in his ear. "I thought you said I needed to get some sleep."

"A kiss," he said gruffly. "Then you can sleep."

So she kissed him.

And that, of course, led to more kisses.

Which led to another thoroughly satisfying hour of lovemaking.

It was after three when they finally went to sleep, and six in the morning when the phone rang again.

"Don't answer that," Jace grumbled in her ear.

More asleep than awake, ignoring her hot new fiancé's wise advice and not stopping to think that the call would probably be someone she didn't really want to talk to without advance preparation, Joss groped for the phone.

"'Lo?" she answered groggily.

"Kenny just called me," her mother said tightly. "He is devastated. He tried not to drag me into this, but what could the poor man do? He spent a sleepless night after he talked to you. And in the end, well, he just couldn't help himself. Jocelyn Marie, you have broken a good man's heart. How could you? I ask you, sincerely, what is the matter with you? Have you lost your mind?"

Joss had dragged herself up against the pillows by then.

She must have had a stricken look on her face because Jace was fully awake and watching her, a frown of concern between his brows.

She put her hand over the mouthpiece and whispered, "My mother."

He must have been holding his breath because he let it out slowly. "You want me to talk to her?"

"Oh, no. Uh-uh. I don't think so…"

"Jocelyn, hello?" Her mother's voice grated in her ear. "Are you there? Can you hear me?"

She took her hand away from the mouthpiece. "I'm here."

Her mother huffed. "I asked you several questions. You didn't answer a single one of them."

"Yes, well, Mom, I didn't know where to start."

"Start by reassuring me that this all just a terrible misunderstanding. Tell me you're not marrying some stranger you just met."

Joss swallowed, sucked in a slow breath and counted to five. Jace held out his hand. Gratefully, she took it and wove her fingers with his.

"Jocelyn, will you please answer me?"

"All right, Mom. No, I am not marrying a stranger. I'm marrying a wonderful man named Jason Traub. Jace and I are buying a business together and staying here in Montana to make a new life for ourselves."

Her mother made a tight, outraged little sound. "So it's all true then, what poor Kenny said? You have gone over the edge, lost your mind completely. This is pure craziness. Now, you listen to me…."

"Mom, I—"

"Jocelyn, I'm begging you. I want you to pack up your things and get a flight home. Now. Today. This instant.

Call me as soon as you have your flight number and I will meet you at the airport on your arrival. We can—"

"No!" Joss pretty much shouted the word. By then, she was clutching Jace's hand for dear life.

"What did you say?" her mother demanded.

"I said no, Mom. No. I am getting married right here, in Thunder Canyon, Montana, on the twenty-eighth of July. That's all there is to it. I hope you'll come for the wedding. But if you don't, well, that's your choice."

Her mother scoffed outright. "But this is ridiculous. Impossible. It's just all wrong."

"I'm sorry you feel that way, Mom. I'm sorry that lately we seem to be unable to communicate in any constructive way. The wedding will take place here at the Thunder Canyon Resort at five in the afternoon, with a reception in the Rib Shack restaurant, also here at the resort, afterward. I love you and I hope you'll come. Goodbye."

As usual, her mom was still talking frantically as she gently set the phone back in its cradle. "Oh, my Lord…."

"Come here, come on." Jace pulled her close.

She wrapped her arms around him good and tight. "Why couldn't I have a normal mother—say, one like yours? That would be so refreshing."

He pressed his lips to the crown of her head. "Your mom will come around in time."

"I hope so. I truly do. She's not *all* bad, you know?"

He answered gently, "I know she's not."

"She really does love me. I think she truly believes that she's doing the right thing. She just can't let go of the idea that Kenny Donovan is a knight in shining armor and I have to be out of my mind to walk away from him." She let out a low groan. "I honestly have no clue how to get through to her."

He tipped her chin up and pressed a quick, hard kiss on

her lips. "I know a copy place on the east side of town, in the mall in what we call New Town. We'll put some invitations together today to send out to the family. We'll send one to your mom, too."

"You think sending her an invitation is going to make a difference with her? Frankly, I can't see how."

He kissed her again, lightly this time. "I just think it's good to remind her that we do want her here for our wedding. By the time she gets the invitation, she'll have had a few days to think it over, to change her mind about coming on so strong. I think once she settles down, she's going to realize that you're what matters to her. She'll want to mend fences by then, to make peace with you."

"Oh, if you could only be right about that."

He stroked her hair. She snuggled in even closer, reveling in the warmth of his body, the strength in his big arms, the scent of him that was clean and manly and managed somehow to excite her and to comfort her simultaneously. He asked, "You want try and get a little more sleep?"

"Hah, as if that's an option at this point. I'm so hopped up on adrenaline, my ears are buzzing."

"So okay, let's get some breakfast."

Over bacon and eggs at the Grubstake, they planned out the day.

It was a busy one.

First they went to the New Town copy shop and ordered some simple, attractive-looking invitations. The clerk said their order would be ready the next day, which was Tuesday.

From the copy shop, they moved on to Lizzie's bakery. Aunt Melba was there, just leaving after enjoying a muffin and morning coffee. She chided them for missing church and then congratulated them on their upcoming wedding.

"Lizzie told me the news and I couldn't be happier about it." She insisted on hugging them both and seized Jace first. Holding him tight against her considerable bosom, she announced, "I am so pleased you'll be making your home right here in Thunder Canyon."

"Uh, thanks, Melba," Jace said, easing free of her grip.

She grabbed Joss next. "Oh, I know you two will be very happy here." Joss managed a noise of agreement as Melba crushed her closer. "And we need more nice, hard-working young people in this town." She took Joss by the shoulders and held her away at last. "Our youth, after all, are our future."

"So true," Joss agreed. "We'll be sending you an invitation. I hope you can come."

"I wouldn't miss it for the world, my dear."

Melba waved as she left them. They ordered a couple of large coffees. Lizzie joined them and they chose the cake they wanted *and* learned that the two-bedroom apartment over the bakery was vacant.

Lizzie said Joss and Jace were welcome to it until they found the house they were looking for. She took them up and showed them the place, which was charming and fully furnished, right down to the linens in the bathroom, the pretty old-fashioned floral-patterned dishes in the kitchen and the impressive array of pots and pans.

Lizzie explained, "I lived here for a while before Ethan and I got married. It's all pretty much as it was when I stayed here. I keep meaning to have a big garage sale, get rid of everything and put it up for rent. But then, you know, it's kind of nice to have it available, just in case someone in the family needs a place to stay…."

"I love it," Joss told her. "It's perfect."

Jace whipped out his checkbook, but Joss told him to put it away. He gave her a dark look.

She didn't back down. "Come on, let me cover this at least. Please?"

He wrapped an arm around her and they shared a quick kiss.

After which Lizzie informed them that she wouldn't take money from either of them. She waved a hand. "No way. You're family. I have a successful business *and* a rich husband. I don't need the money. Just take good care of the place, that's all I ask."

Both Joss and Jace promised that they would.

The three of them sat in the apartment's bright living room overlooking Main Street and chatted for a while. Jace told Lizzie about their plans to buy the Hitching Post *and* a new home. Lizzie suggested Bonnie Drake for their Realtor. She said that both she and Ethan had worked with Bonnie before.

But Jace told her that the Drake woman was representing the owner of the Hitching Post and he would rather use someone else. Lizzie whipped out the business card of a guy who came in the bakery every morning early for breakfast.

"His name is Milo Quinn," she said. "An older guy. Seems nice. Steady and dependable. I think you'll like him."

They went to the county courthouse next to see about getting their marriage license. It was a relatively simple procedure, although in Montana, the bride was required to have a test for rubella before the license could be issued. Jace had the solution to that one. He called the family doctor—his brother Dillon—and they drove over to Dillon's clinic to get the test done.

That afternoon, they met with Milo at his office. Tall and white-haired, he wore a Western-cut sport coat, dark brown slacks and tooled boots. He set up an appointment for them to see the Hitching Post the next day. He also said he would find them some houses on acreage.

After that, they returned to the resort and spoke with Grant, who congratulated them on their upcoming wedding and said that he was certain Chef Roarke would be happy to cater their reception. He took them upstairs to meet with Shane. He was agreeable. They set an appointment for 9:00 a.m. on Wednesday to get the menu planned.

And then they went back to Dillon Traub's clinic to pick up the expedited rubella test results. They made it to the county clerk's office again before it closed. When they left the courthouse, they had their license.

That night, they were so tired that they made love only once.

And they were up bright and early Tuesday morning. They grabbed a quick breakfast and went down into town to meet Milo Quinn at the Hitching Post.

Joss loved the bar and grill from the first moment she stepped through the front door. It was as rustic inside as out and had an old-timey feel about it, with the dining room on one side and the bar on the other. There was plenty of space for a dance floor on the bar side and a small stage in the corner where a band could set up. No wonder the place had always been a hit with the locals. It was a great venue. As long as she and Jace provided good food and good service, they probably couldn't go wrong.

Jace was relieved to discover that the painting of the Shady Lady still hung in the place of honor above the gorgeous antique bar. "She is lookin' way hot as always," Jace said with a grin.

Milo assured them that the painting and all the furnishings and equipment were part of the very reasonable asking price. Lance O'Doherty's daughter, it seemed, really wanted to sell. The place had a full, if somewhat dated, restaurant-style kitchen. And off the long hallway in the back, there were restrooms and three smaller dining rooms for private parties.

The building could use some updating—of the kitchen and of the restrooms. The main bar and restaurant could stand a little sprucing, too. The idea was to keep all that old-time Hitching Post charm, but freshen things up, make it brighter and more inviting.

All three of them went for lunch together at a pizza place in New Town and then they followed Milo out to see a trio of four- to five-acre properties. None of them were quite what they were looking for.

That evening, they met Lizzie and Ethan for dinner in the resort's Gallatin Room. Over thick, perfectly seared filets, garlic potatoes and curried spinach, they discussed the potential purchase of the bar and grill. Lizzie and Ethan both offered advice.

Shane Roarke emerged from the kitchen while they were devouring a to-die-for dessert of carrot cake and sweet pea ice cream with lavender caramel sauce. The chef greeted Joss and Jason, who introduced him to Jace's brother and his wife. Shane stayed to make small talk for a few minutes and then moved on.

Ethan stared after him. "That guy reminds me of someone…."

Joss and Jason both laughed. Joss said, "We had the same feeling the first time we saw him. We just can't figure out exactly *who* he reminds us of."

The food for the reception, they decided when they met with Shane the next morning, would be buffet-style. They went with mostly finger foods. From the resort, they drove to Milo Quinn's office. After lengthy discussion, Jace offered the asking price on the Hitching Post.

Once they signed the offer, they picked up their invitations at the copy place and returned to the resort, where they spent a few hours scrolling the address lists stored in their smartphones, filling out the envelopes and sticking on stamps. Joss stuck a little note in the invitation to her mother. The note explained that she and Jace had found an apartment to live in until they chose a new home. She gave her mom the address and the phone number at the new place, although she really wasn't expecting to hear from her mother anytime soon—and not expecting her to come to the wedding either.

Every time she thought of her mom, a gray, sad gloom descended. It was a giant rift that had opened up between them over that jackass Kenny Donovan. Joss appreciated Jace's positive attitude about the situation, but she doubted she and her mom would be making peace for a long time to come.

Jace looked up from the envelope he was addressing. "That was a really sad-sounding sigh."

She pulled a face. "It's just, you know, my mother..."

He reached across the table and put his hand over hers. "Hey, she'll come around."

She turned her hand over and clasped his. And then she got up from her seat so she could lean close to him and share a slow, sweet kiss.

Later, they took the finished invitations down to the front desk where the clerk promised they would go out with the morning mail. Back in the suite, they ordered room service. Shandie Traub called. She invited them to dinner the next night, which was great. They wouldn't have to worry about stocking the cupboards at the apartment on their first day there.

It was their final night in the king-sized pillow-top bed. They made the most of it, enjoying slow, lazy love for hour upon hour.

As always, it was the best. Better than ever, Joss thought, as she sat in his lap, facing him, her legs wrapped around him, holding him deep within her.

Oh, yes! Better every time. Who knew it could be like this? Really, she'd had no idea.

He surged up into her. And she took him. Deeper. All the way. He filled her up so perfectly.

She cried his name. He kissed her, his mouth claiming hers so hungrily as she felt his climax take him.

Seconds later, she joined him. They went over the edge of the world together.

This, she thought. *Yes! Nothing like this. Ever. Not ever in my life before…*

Grant had told them they didn't need to be out of the suite until noon, so they stayed in bed later than usual Thursday morning.

At nine-thirty, as they were lazily dozing and Joss was telling herself they really needed to get motivated and get their stuff packed to move over to the apartment, the phone rang.

Jace said what he always said: "Don't answer that."

And she did what she always did. "'Lo?"

"Is this Jocelyn?"

She sat bolt-upright.

Jace sat up, too. "What the—"

"It's Milo," she whispered excitedly. Then she cleared her throat and tried to sound composed. "Hi, Milo. What's up?"

"You've just bought the Hitching Post," the Realtor announced.

Joss let out a yell and pumped her fist toward the ceiling.

"Give me that." Jace took the phone. "Hey, Milo…"

Milo said something. Jace listened and finally answered, "Great. We'll be there." He handed her the phone back.

She put it to her ear, but the Realtor had already hung up. "He's gone." She dropped the phone back on the cradle. "So?"

"We're meeting him at his office at three today to sign the final agreement, give him the earnest money check and talk about inspections. He also said that if everything goes as planned, we close on the property August fifteenth."

"So fast!"

"It's a little over thirty days. That's about right."

She sat there, mouth agape, heart racing with excitement. "Jace, we did it. This is happening. It's really, really happening."

He chuckled, "No kidding."

She swayed his way and planted a big, smacking kiss in the middle of his broad, handsome forehead. He tried to reach for her, but she ducked back, giggling.

"Get back here," he growled.

"No way. I can't sit still." She shoved off the covers and leaped from the bed.

Jace started to go after her, but then changed his mind. He laced his hands behind his head and grinned—possibly because she was totally naked. "All right," he said. "Have it your way. I gotta admit I'm lovin' the view from here."

She let out another joyous shout and then she grabbed her robe from the floor where she'd dropped it the night before. Quickly, she tugged it on and tied the sash. Then she ran around the room chanting, "We did it, we did it, we bought the Hitching Post!"

He just sat there, beaming. "Gee, Joss. You could show a little excitement, don't you think?"

With a long trill of laughter, she ran back to the bed,

grabbed her pillow and began hitting him over the head with it. "Oh, this is fabulous! Oh, I just can't believe it…."

"Hey," he protested, still laughing. "Knock that off." He grabbed for the pillow and snatched it away from her. Then he used it against her, trying to bop her a good one.

She played along, leaning in as he took aim, then jumping out of the way when he delivered a blow. "You missed! I'm too fast for you."

He clutched the pillow against his rock-hard, gorgeous chest so she couldn't steal it back from him and threatened in the raspy voice of a villain in some old-time melodrama, "That's it for you, beautiful."

"Hah!"

The bad-guy leer vanished. He gave her the bedroom eyes and crooked his index finger. "Come down here. Nice and close…"

"Forget that noise, mister!" Breathing fast, her heart racing with giddy excitement, she started laughing again.

And then, just like that, out of nowhere, her breath caught.

She could not breathe and her heart had stopped stock-still in her chest.

Twin lines appeared between Jace's dark brows. "Joss, you okay?"

She *was* actually. More than okay.

The breath came flooding back into her chest and her heart started beating again and the hotel bedroom seemed so beautiful suddenly. It seemed to glow with golden light. *Happy*, she thought. *At this moment, I am so perfectly, gloriously happy.* Never in her life had she felt exactly like this. Everything just paled next to this.

She saw it all, her life up till now: her lonely childhood with her brave, determined, damaged mother. Her adolescence, during all of which she'd felt awkward and different;

she'd never managed to fit in. And later, through a couple of years of college and her first job in the restaurant business, which she'd discovered she enjoyed. Through her search for a good guy who could help her make the big, loud happy family she'd always dreamed of. To Kenny, who was supposed to be the one, her guy forever, and had turned out to be anything but.

All of it. The whole of her life until she met Jace. It simply couldn't compare to her days and nights with him, to this one shining, perfect moment.

She didn't stop to consider. She just opened her mouth and let the scary words pour out. "I love you, Jason Traub. I love you so much. I never knew that it could be like this, that it could *feel* like this, could fill me up like this, I…" Her throat clogged and the words ran out.

He didn't look happy.

Not in the least. He looked…stunned maybe?

And very uncomfortable.

She felt her face turn blazing red. "Oh, wow." She winced. "More information than you needed, huh?"

Because seriously, hadn't he made it painfully clear upfront that he had no clue what love was, that he just didn't get it and didn't care to get it? That he only wanted to start a business and settle down. That he liked her a lot, but for him, love didn't enter into it.

How had he put it last Sunday when he asked her to marry him?

I have no idea what love really is and I'm better off not kidding myself that I do….

Oh, God. Way to go, Joss. What had possessed her to just blurt it out like that?

He set the pillow aside and sucked in a slow breath. "Uh. Well. Good." And he actually pasted on this fake, too-cheerful smile. "That's great, Joss. I mean, thank you."

"Thank you?"

"Aw, Joss..."

"I say I love you and you say 'Thank you'?"

"Joss..."

She put up a hand. "Okay. Yeah. Bad. Really bad." And exactly what she should have expected, if she'd only had the presence of mind to keep her mouth shut until she'd thought the whole thing through. Duh. Double duh in a big, big way.

"Come on, Joss..." He looked so embarrassed, so totally out of his depth.

And she? Her mouth felt dry as a handful of dust. Her heart felt like a shriveled husk in her chest. She swallowed. With care. And she made herself ask him, "So then, is this going to ruin it for you? Do you want to back out? Because if you do, I would appreciate knowing that now."

"Back out?" He looked totally dazed, beyond confused. And so handsome, she hated him.

Almost as much as she loved him.

Because seriously, he was much too good to look at. It wasn't fair, now she thought about it, how really hot he was. "Excuse me," she said carefully, "are you saying you didn't understand the question?"

He started to push back the covers. "Joss, I—"

"Uh-uh." She leveled a look on him that had him sinking back into the bed. "Do you want to back out? Just say so. Just answer the question."

"No, then. Okay?"

Okay? As a matter of fact, it wasn't. It wasn't okay in the least. "No," she echoed with excruciating care.

"No," he repeated yet again. "It's what I said."

"No, you don't understand? Or no, you don't want to marry me? What are you telling me, Jace? Just do me a big favor and be straight with me about this."

His handsome, square jaw was set. He said, with heavy emphasis, "I *do* want to marry you. I *don't* want to back out."

Relief flooded through her. Yeah, it was tinged with the weight of sadness and mortification and a host of other not-so-fun emotions. But still, it was something. "You mean that? You really do still want to marry me?"

Now he was the one swallowing. She watched his Adam's apple bounce. And then he nodded. "I do. Yeah, it's what I want. You and me. The life we planned. I still want that." He paused. She waited. Finally, he began again, haltingly, "It's just that, well, the whole love thing—"

She cut him off. "Stop. I don't want to hear it, you know? I sincerely do not."

He blew out a slow, cheek-puffing breath. "Wow. Well. Whatever you say."

She wrapped her arms around herself in a meager attempt to give herself the comfort he couldn't—or wouldn't. "It was…a mistake. To even bring it up, the whole love thing. I know that. I don't know what I was thinking. After all, I understand how you feel about it. And it's my bad. It's not like you didn't set me straight right from the first, not like you didn't make yourself perfectly clear."

"Joss…"

She shook her head. Hard. "No, I mean it. Can we just stop talking about it? Can we just let it go?"

Was that relief she saw in those beautiful chocolate-brown eyes of his?

So what if it was? She could relate. They were both relieved—he that she was giving up the love talk, she because he claimed he still wanted to marry her.

Now her mouth tasted like sawdust. And the luxurious bedroom, aglow with golden light moments before, was all at once dingy and dark.

"Joss, you know that I care for you."

She looked away. "Just don't, okay? Just stop. I said I understand. And I do. There's nothing more to say about it."

The covers rustled as he pushed them aside again. "Damn it, Joss…"

Someone knocked on the outer door.

It was perfect timing as far as Joss was concerned. "What now?" she asked bleakly, turning to look at him again. "You think that's your mother?"

He swung his feet to the floor. God, he was so beautiful. "I hope not," he muttered. "I'll get rid of her."

"No, I'll get it." She tied the belt of her robe more securely.

He didn't say anything. He was looking at her sideways, a concerned kind of look.

Well, he could take that look and shove it. She didn't need his concern. He didn't want to go there—and neither did she. Not anymore. They got along great and they knew what they wanted and that was enough for him.

And it would damn well be enough for her. To show him she was fine with the way things were, she sent him a big, defiant smile, after which she whirled and headed for the other room, pausing only to shut the bedroom door firmly behind her.

The knock came again as she reached the foyer. She ran her hand back through her sleep-mussed hair and peeked through the peephole.

Her heart sank. It wasn't Jace's mom out there in the hallway.

It was hers.

Chapter Twelve

With a low moan, Joss rested her forehead against the suite's thick outer door. She did not want to open it. She really, really didn't.

Shutting her eyes, she sucked in a slow breath, peeled herself off the door and fled back to the bedroom.

When she flung the door wide, she found Jace right where she'd left him, sitting on the edge of the bed, wearing nothing but a slight frown.

One look at her expression and he jumped to his feet. "What? Who is it?"

She let out a groan. "You'd better get dressed."

"What's going on?"

"It's my mother."

He dropped back to the edge of the bed. "Wait a minute. Your mother. Here at the resort?"

She nodded. As if on cue, her mother knocked for the third time, five swift, hard raps on the outer door.

Jace jumped up again and came for her. Before she could think to jerk away, he caught her face between his hands. "It's okay. It'll be okay."

"Oh, I'm so glad one of us thinks so." She bit back a sob. His touch felt so good. As good as ever. Was that right? Was that fair?

And then he kissed her, the lightest brushing breath of a kiss. That felt good, too. It comforted her in spite of everything. "Now you go on, let her in," he said gently. "I'll put some clothes on."

She laughed, a slightly wild sound. "Great idea. Ahem. I mean, you know. That you should get dressed..." God, she was babbling. Losing it. Holding on to composure by the tiniest of threads.

"There's nothing to worry about," he said. "It's good that she's here."

"Good?" she whispered desperately. "How can it be good?"

"Well, because it means that you two can work everything out now, all the stuff that's been tearing you apart."

"But I...she's not...we can't..." She sputtered into silence.

"It's okay," he said again. "Go let her in." He took her shoulders, turned her around and gave her a gentle push.

She went. What choice did she have?

Quietly, he shut the bedroom door behind her.

And she kept walking, one foot in front of the other, across the living area, back into the foyer, right up to the outer door. She undid the chain, turned the dead bolt.

And pulled the door back. "Mom, hi." RaeEllen had her two large black rolling suitcases, one to either side of her. She planned on a long stay apparently, "It's, um, good to see you," Joss said. She leaned forward and kissed her mother's cheek. Then she stepped back so her mom could enter.

Glancing suspiciously from side to side, RaeEllen crossed the threshold, pulling one of the suitcases behind her.

Joss stepped around her and brought in the other one. She shut the door. "This is…a surprise."

RaeEllen settled her favorite brown purse more comfortably on the shoulder of her cream-colored summer blazer. "You're not even dressed? At this hour? It's almost ten."

Joss kept her smile in place. "Just leave your purse on the table there. And come on into the living area. Things have been so busy. There's so much to do in such a short time." She was babbling again, and she knew it. But somehow, she couldn't seem to stop herself. "We just heard a few minutes ago that we bought the restaurant we offered on and we're very excited that the deal went through, that our plans are—"

"A restaurant? You *bought* a restaurant?"

"Yes, we did. We're so excited. And we've been looking for a house, *and* getting the invitations out, *and* finding a place to stay in the interim. Plus there's all the wedding stuff—arranging for the cake and settling on the menu. It goes on and on. Today's another big day because we'll be moving to—"

"We?" Her mother's pale blue eyes widened.

"Yeah. Jason, my fiancé, and me. We have to be out of the suite by noon and we're moving temporarily to an apartment down in town. I sent you a note about that, along with a wedding invitation. But of course, you didn't get it yet. And anyway, we were both worn out with all the running around, pulling everything together, so we decided to indulge ourselves and sleep in a little. We were tired, you know? Just beat."

RaeEllen held on to her brown bag for dear life and blinked several times in rapid succession. "He's here, in this room, with you?"

"That's right." Joss reminded herself not to clench her teeth. "Jason's in the bedroom actually. He's getting dressed."

"Oh. Getting dressed. Then you're telling me he…well, I mean, that you and he…"

Joss had had enough. "Come on, Mom. Stop acting like the parson's wife in some Jane Austen novel. Yes, not only are Jace and I getting married, we are already living together. And it's working out great." *Well, except for the fact that I love him and he* doesn't *love me….*

"It's working out great," RaeEllen repeated in a tone that said it didn't sound the least great to her.

"Yes, that's what I said. We're very happy together."

"But you hardly know this man and only three weeks ago you were supposed to have married Kenny, who is deeply, deeply hurt by your desertion, who only wants a chance to make you happy, to—"

"Mom. Whoa. Stop." Joss waved both her hands in front of her mother's face. "This is kind of a loop we're into here, Mom. Can we please stop going round and round about things we've already discussed and don't seem capable of coming to any agreement on?"

Her mother's mouth drew painfully tight. "Of course. Whatever you say."

Joss focused on her mother's words and tried her best to ignore the angry, disapproving tone. "Thank you. I appreciate that." She straightened her robe, an action that, for some reason, caused her mother to gasp. Joss was trying to figure out what exactly that gasp meant when RaeEllen reached out and grabbed her hand—her left hand.

"Lovely." Her mother sounded sincere as she studied Joss's engagement ring.

Joss tried to tell herself that maybe there was hope for the situation after all, that her mom might actually try to make the best of things. "Oh, I know. I love it."

RaeEllen glanced up, and delivered the zinger. "It looks real."

That did it. Joss withdrew her hand. "I'm not kidding, Mom. I know you've had a long trip and I would like to be glad you've come, but I've had enough."

"What does that mean?"

"It means I'm not going to sit still and let you run over me. I'm not a little girl anymore. I'm a grown woman and I get to determine the direction of my own life, which you *used* to understand perfectly. Either you start *behaving* in a civil manner and treat me like an adult again, or you can just roll those suitcases right out the door and head for home."

Her mother looked stricken. "But I drove all the way here. As you've already mentioned, it was a very long trip and I'm exhausted."

"Then you'd better stop with the mean remarks, hadn't you? Or you'll be on the road again."

RaeEllen assumed an injured air. "You don't want me here? Is that what you're telling me?"

Joss tried valiantly to form an answer to that one. But what could she say? The truth was she *didn't* want her mother there. Not unless she changed her tune.

RaeEllen spoke again, more gently. "It's only, well, I felt I should come. I felt we should…work out our differences."

"And that's admirable, Mom." Warily, she eyed the two

large suitcases. "So…you were thinking you would stay right through to the wedding?"

Her mother pressed her lips together and nodded sharply. "As long as it takes, yes. I have some family leave stored up."

Joss was stuck back there with that first sentence. "As long as what takes?"

Her mother smoothed her short, fine brown hair. "I wonder, could I have a glass of water?"

Joss resisted the overwhelming desire to lay down the law. She'd already made herself more than clear. Going into it all again right this moment would only be hooking back into the loop she'd accused her mother of falling into. "Of course," she finally said. "Come on into the living area."

"My suitcases…"

"Just leave them here for now." She turned to enter the main area of the suite, her mother close on her heels. "Have a seat." She gestured at the sofa and went to the wet bar, where she filled a glass with ice and opened one of the complimentary bottles of spring water.

Jace appeared, fully dressed in nice jeans, a knit shirt and the usual high-dollar boots. He went straight to her mother. "Mrs. Bennings, hello." He laid on the Texas charm, bowing a little at the waist as he reached across the coffee table. "How great to meet you."

Even her sour-hearted mom couldn't completely resist him. She gave him her hand. He cradled it between his two larger ones, and he hit her with one of those ladykiller smiles of his, the kind that could break a woman's heart at twenty paces.

Her mom sniffed. "It's Ms. Bennings, thank you." Delicately, she withdrew her hand.

Joss hurried to Jace's rescue. "But only to strangers."

Jace straightened and slid her a questioning look. Blithely, she went on, "Of course, *you'll* call her RaeEllen." She gave her mother a steely-eyed glance. "Unless you'd prefer 'Mom'?"

"Ahem. Well." RaeEllen nodded at Jace. "Yes. RaeEllen, of course. So nice to meet you." Joss set the glass of ice and bottle of water in front of her. "Thank you, Jocelyn."

Joss nodded, and dropped the bomb on poor Jace. "Mom is planning to stay until the wedding."

Carefully, her mother poured the water over the ice. She said nothing.

Jace said, "Ah. Well, that's great." His smile had slipped a little.

Joss watched him, her heart twisting. She loved him. And he didn't do love.

And now her mother was here with that strange, determined look in her hazel eyes. That couldn't be good.

But she could deal with her mother—if only things didn't go wrong with Jace.

He'd said he still wanted the life they had planned.

But did he really?

Had her passionate declaration changed everything for him? Was he second-guessing now, thinking about how he wasn't really the marrying kind after all? That this was all a big mistake, the two of them? That it had happened much too fast, with her on the rebound—and maybe him, too, when you came right down to it. Because there had been that rich oilman's daughter, Tricia. Even though he said it wasn't love with Tricia, well, he *had* proposed to her. And she'd said no.

And he'd gone into something of a depression after that.

So was he maybe now seeing the future they'd been planning as another trap he needed to escape? Was he…

No.

Uh-uh.

She was not going there.

He'd said straight to her face that he still wanted to marry her. If he'd changed his mind, he could have just said so. She'd given him an opening. A really *wide* opening.

And he'd refused to take it.

If he wanted out, he could tell her. He was a grown man fully capable of speaking his mind.

But what if I *want out now? What if* I've *decided I don't want a marriage without love?*

She turned those painful questions over in her mind, and realized that it *wouldn't* be a loveless marriage. At least not on her end.

And she didn't want to back out. Not on her life. She wanted Jace and she wanted everything he offered her—wanted her dream, just as she'd always imagined it might be. Especially now that her dream would include the most important part: the man she loved. He said he still wanted to live her dream with her.

She would have to be crazy to turn her back on that. And she wouldn't. No way.

She let out a heavy sigh.

And realized that both Jace and her mother were staring at her—Jace kind of nervously, her mom in a measuring, calculating way.

Fine. Let 'em stare. "Mom, there's a second bedroom at the apartment where Jace and I will be staying until we find a house. You're welcome to it." She caught Jace's eye and challenged, "Right, Jace?"

She had to give him credit. He didn't even flinch. "Absolutely. RaeEllen, we'd be happy to have you stay with us."

Whatever her mother's real agenda, she had the grace

to hesitate. "Really, I can get a hotel room. I don't want to impose."

Jace stepped right up. "It's no imposition, RaeEllen. You're family, after all."

Milo Quinn's office was only a few blocks from the Mountain Bluebell Bakery and the apartment above it, so Joss and Jason walked to their three o'clock appointment.

An hour later, they left Milo's office with a signed contract on the Hitching Post. Clouds had gathered in the wide Montana sky when they emerged onto Pine Street. A few random drops started falling as they strolled north to Main.

Jace glanced up at the gray underbelly of the thick cloud cover. "We'd better get moving or we're going to get wet."

So they ran around the corner and down the block. They ducked through the bakery's front door just as the sky opened up and the downpour began. One of Lizzie's employees gave them a smile and a wave as they headed up the stairs to the apartment above.

She got to there first. The doorknob wouldn't turn. She sighed. "My mom's used to city life. She's locked herself in." She raised her hand to knock.

Jace caught her wrist before her knuckles connected with the door. "We have to talk." His voice was so deep and more than a little rough.

Her heart did something unsettling inside her chest. And her skin felt all tingly and warm. Her breath snagging in her throat, she turned to him, met those dark velvet eyes that burned into hers, smelled the spicy, green, electric scent that belonged to only him….

"Talk? About what?" She was pleased that aside from a certain huskiness, her voice betrayed none of her excitement. She didn't *want* to be excited by him. Not now.

Not with her new—and unreturned—love so fresh and raw within her.

He looked at her steadily. "It's not the same. You're… distant. Cool to me."

She shrugged. "Be patient. I'll get over it." She wouldn't. But she would get used to it—at least she hoped she would. She'd learn to live with being alone in love.

His gaze burned darker, more intense. "Listen, do you need me to say it? I can just say it if it's what you need."

She took his meaning and whispered low, "You would say that you love me, even though you don't?"

"It's only words."

"To you maybe."

He still held her wrist. And didn't let go. Instead, he guided it back behind her and brought her up close against his broad, rocklike chest. "Whatever you want. Just say it. I'll do it."

Her breasts felt oversensitive, pressing as they did into the hardness and heat of him. Her body burned. And her heart…

It ached. A deep, thick kind of ache. An ache that was almost pleasurable. She didn't have his love. But he did want her. A lot. It was something. Not enough, but still. Better than nothing.

"Okay, Jace. You go ahead. You say it. You lie to me."

His arm banded tighter and he pulled her even closer. What breath she had left came out in a gasp.

And then he said it, roughly, angrily, his breath warm and sweet across her cheek. "I love you, Joss."

She tipped her head to the side, opened her mouth slightly and ran her tongue over her upper lip, openly taunting him. His eyes burned brighter and a muscle jumped in his jaw. "Hmm," she said with a smile that wasn't really a smile at all. "Somehow it doesn't have the ring of truth, you know? And what good is a lie to me? Not a whole lot."

"Joss..." He said her name very low that time. It was a warning. And also, somehow, a plea. "I just don't want to lose you over this, okay? Over three little words. How stupid would that be? No, I don't get the whole love thing. I think it's a crock. You want to be with someone, build a life with someone, or you don't. And the point is, I want a life with you. And you want the same thing with me."

She hitched her chin higher. "I'm not arguing. We're on the same page with this."

"Are we?" He didn't look convinced.

And she was softening. How could she help it, with his fine, big body pressed against hers, tempting her? And his heated words in her ears, reminding her that he did care, that he wanted her, that he had promised to be a true husband to her. And that she believed him on all those points, believed *in* him.

The L-word shouldn't matter so much. It was what a person *did* that mattered.

"Yes." She let her tone go soft as her heart. "Yes, we're on the same page." She reached up with the hand he hadn't trapped behind her back and caressed the slightly stubbled line of his so-manly jaw. "We just bought our business. We're going to find the right house. We're getting married and we're going to have as many kids as the good Lord will grant us."

"It's gonna be great," he said fervently, the contract in his free hand crackling a little as he tightened his fist on it. "You'll see."

"I know." She gave him a real smile that time, even if it was a little wobbly. "Yes, it will be. Great."

"Joss..." He whispered her name as his fine mouth swooped down to cover hers.

Her knees went loose and she sagged back heavily against the door. Oh, that mouth of his—it played over hers, hitting every sweet, hot, perfect note. It was a symphony he created, every time he kissed her. Slow and tempting, fast and hot. He varied the notes and the rhythms. He swept her away on a warm tide of pleasure. She sighed and surrendered to the spell that he wove.

And then, just she was sliding her free hand up to clasp his neck and pull him even closer, the door behind her gave way.

With a sharp little cry, she stumbled backward.

"What the..." Jace growled.

Somehow, she managed to stay on her feet. She whirled to find her mother standing there, hazel eyes wide with pretended surprise.

"Oh!" RaeEllen exclaimed. "Well, I'm sorry. I thought I heard a knock...."

"Not a problem," Joss lied, as she straightened her light summer shirt and recovered her dignity.

Jace actually chuckled. "Caught us in the act, RaeEllen."

RaeEllen only pinched up her mouth and smoothed her hair. "I'm glad you're back. I've made a list of the staples we absolutely must have to function around here. And Jason, I was thinking that maybe you could make a quick run to the local supermarket while Jocelyn and I finish putting our things away."

Joss saw right through her mother. It was divide and conquer time. She was sending Jace away so she could go to work on Joss. Not happening. "We can deal with that later, Mom. We're invited to dinner at Jace's cousin Dax's house tonight."

"But we'll at least need eggs and coffee for breakfast tomorrow."

"Actually, we won't. We can just walk downstairs to the bakery. The breakfast croissants have eggs, ham, sausage—whatever you want in them. And they are to die for."

"That could get expensive."

"Mom, it's one day. We'll shop for food tomorrow, after breakfast, when it's not pouring down rain."

Jace spoke up. "Give me the list, RaeEllen. I'll be happy to pick up what we need right now."

Joss whirled on him. "We should talk." She grabbed his hand. "Come in the bedroom." She sent her mother a withering glance. "Mom, we'll be right back."

RaeEllen knew when to keep her mouth shut. She gave a tight little smile and let them go.

Jace went willingly enough. Joss towed him to the larger bedroom at the back of the apartment, dragged him inside and shut the door.

He went over and dropped to the edge of the old-fashioned double bed with its dark headboard and bright log cabin quilt.

She stayed near the door. "You know what she's doing, don't you?"

He didn't even have to think about it. "She wants to get you alone and tell you all the reasons you shouldn't marry me."

"So why are you letting her get away with it?"

"Because you can't avoid her forever. She's staying right here in the apartment with us. You might as well face her down at the gate, let her know you're not running scared and she'd better straighten up and fly right or she can get back in that big old Buick of hers and head home to Sacramento."

He was right, of course.

But still. "I *have* let her know. It doesn't do any good."

"So tell her to go home."

"I'm…not at that point yet. Close. But not yet."

He got up then. He came to her, clasping her shoulders between his strong hands. "You need to show her she doesn't get to you."

"But that's just it. She *does* get to me—and don't tell me you don't know exactly what I'm going through here. Remember that first day we met? When you practically begged me to go to the Rib Shack with you, to pretend to be your date so your family would stop trying to set you up?"

He grunted. "You *would* have to remind me. They were driving me nuts."

"So all right, then. You understand. And I mean it. Don't leave me alone with her."

"Joss, you're only putting off the inevitable."

"That's right. I keep hoping I'll get lucky and she'll decide to back off and be reasonable."

He shook his head. "She seems pretty determined."

She made a face at him. "She's determined, all right. Determined to put a stop to our wedding. Think about that. Out on the landing a few minutes ago, you were all about how you really, really do want to marry me."

"It's true," he said simply. "I do want to marry you."

His words touched her. He was such a big, handsome bundle of contradictions. He couldn't say the L-word without scowling. Yet he sincerely wanted to make a life with her.

"My mother is up to no good," she said.

"Joss, she came all the way here to Montana to try and make it up with you."

She wrinkled her nose at him. "That is so not what she's here for."

He caught a lock of her hair, rubbed it between his fingers. "Talk to her."

She could become seriously annoyed with him. "When

it's *your* mother, you can't run away fast enough. But when it's *my* mom, I'm supposed to hold my ground and talk it out."

"You're a woman. Women are better at all that crap."

"Crap," she muttered. "A truer word was never spoken."

He slid his hand up under her hair and clasped her nape. Lovely sensations cascaded through her. And then he pressed his lips so tenderly to hers. "Talk to her."

Five minutes later, he was out the door.

And she was alone with her scheming mother, who took her hands and dragged her into the long, narrow kitchen and down to the little round table at the far end.

"Sit down," RaeEllen said in her warmest, most conciliatory tones. "Let's catch up a little…."

Reluctantly, Joss sat.

"Jason is very handsome," her mother said carefully, a brave soldier in a dangerous field of hair-trigger land mines. "Very charming and very…compelling."

"Yes, he is."

"And I gather he's got money."

"Yes, he does."

"I can understand how he might have swept you off your feet." RaeEllen paused. Presumably so that Joss could agree with her.

Joss said nothing.

Her mother forged on. "But really, how can he possibly be in love with you, or you with him?"

Love. Joss felt the muscles between her shoulder blades snap tight. The last thing she wanted to discuss with her mother was love. It was way too sensitive a subject right then.

And she didn't want her mother to know that. RaeEllen was trolling for weaknesses. Joss refused to show her any. She ordered those tense muscles to relax and she kept her face composed.

RaeEllen kept going, rattling off her list of reasons that Joss and Jace were doomed to failure as a couple. "You met so recently. It's just…well, Jocelyn, it's a fling. On the rebound. And the last thing a woman should ever do is marry a man with whom she is having an affair on the rebound."

Joss couldn't resist. She got in a jab of her own. "Is that what happened with you and my father?"

RaeEllen stiffened. "I beg your pardon. We are not discussing your father."

"I'm just trying to determine how you're such an expert on affairs and flings and getting something going on the rebound. The way I remember it, there was just my father. And when he left, that was pretty much it for you."

"Jocelyn, this is not about me."

Joss let out a slow breath and shook her head. "Mom, you're wrong. I think this is very much about you. About you and your fears and your inability to move on, to try again with a man after Dad walked out."

"No. No, it's not." RaeEllen put a hand to her chest. Two bright spots of color had bloomed on her cheeks. "It most certainly is not. This is about you. About the wonderful man who loves you and forgives you for making a fool of him in front of three hundred people on your wedding day."

"I did not make a fool of Kenny. He did that to himself by rolling around half-naked with my own cousin in the coat room of the church."

"That never happened."

"Mom, it happened. I saw it with my own eyes."

"What happened is that you got cold feet. I remember that you were having second thoughts. You confided in me, don't you recall?"

"Yes, I do recall. Quite clearly. You convinced me that

all brides have second thoughts and I should go through with the wedding. You blew me off."

"No, I did not. I helped you to see that you shouldn't let your unfounded fears get in the way of your happiness."

Joss braced an elbow on the table and rested her forehead in her hand. "This is going nowhere."

"We need to talk about this."

"We *have* talked about this. I have no idea why you're so obsessed with convincing me to get back together with a self-absorbed jerk who cheated on me on our wedding day. But I can't argue with you about this any longer. I am finished. I am marrying Jace and I'm never going near Kenny Donovan again and that's the end of it."

"But you—"

"The end of it, Mom. It's over. Stop."

"But I have to—"

Joss dropped her hand flat, smacking the table. The sound was loud and sharp in the small space. "Enough. I've had it. I can't take this any longer. I'm sorry I can't get through to you. And it doesn't matter what you do, you are not going to change my mind."

"Kenny loves you. He loves you so much. And you are cruel and cold to him. How can you be like that? Why can't you see how horribly you're behaving?"

It was the final straw. "That's it. The end. I want you to go back to Sacramento, Mom. I want you out of this apartment. I've got sixteen days until Jace and I get married. They are going to be busy days. I can't have you at me every chance you get, battering away at me, so sure of your righteousness, so certain that eventually you will wear me down. You *won't* wear me down. What you'll do is ruin what should be a beautiful, busy, exciting two weeks."

"You just want me out of here so you can be alone with that man."

Joss let out a laugh that sounded more like a groan. "You know what? That's right. I do want to be alone with Jace. Why wouldn't I want to be alone with him? Jace is funny and tender and smart." *Even if he isn't in love with me.* "And all he wants is to give me the life I've always dreamed of. What's not to like about that, Mom?"

"What happens when he gets tired of you?"

That hurt. That really hurt. She answered firmly. "He wants to be with me. He's not going to get *tired* of me."

"You are blind. Foolish and blind."

Back at ya, Mom. "I mean it. I want you to go."

Jace returned at twenty after five, his arms loaded with groceries. "There are more in the car. Where's your mom?"

"In her room. Sulking." She took one of the bags from him and turned for the kitchen. "She'll be leaving tomorrow morning." He followed her in there and they set the bags on the counter.

He asked, low-voiced so there was no chance her mother might hear, "You're sending her away?"

"Yes, I am."

"You sure?"

"Yes. I'll make it clear she's still welcome to come for the wedding."

He took her hand, turned it over, wove his fingers with hers. "You okay?"

What happens when you get tired of me? "I've been better."

He pulled her close, into the circle of those powerful arms. She let herself lean on him, breathed in the special scent that belonged only to him, told herself that she wasn't going to let her mother's cruel, misguided words get to her.

But those words were in her head now. Stuck there.

Along with the bald facts: She loved him and he didn't love her.

He'd told her right up front that he'd always been a player, that he'd never been one to settle down, not until his whirlwind affair with the rich oilman's daughter. And now, he was doing it again, with her, with Joss.

Could a man really change that much? Or was this just some phase he was going through? He *thought* he ought to settle down, so he'd swept her off her feet and then proposed, just like he'd done with Tricia Lavelle.

He was the last single guy in his family. Maybe that was getting to him. Maybe he was trying to conform to his family's idea of what a man was supposed to do with his life.

Was it only a matter of time before he realized that marriage and a big house full of rowdy kids wasn't for him after all?

The questions spun round and round in her head. She told herself to ignore them. She wasn't going to let them ruin her happiness.

She held on to Jace tighter. It was going to be all right with them. He wouldn't get tired of her. She believed in him, in what they had together.

Everything would work out fine….

Chapter Thirteen

RaeEllen refused to go with them to Dax and Shandie's that night. She said she was tired and needed her rest. "After all," she added loftily, "I have another long drive facing me tomorrow."

Joss didn't try to change her mind. If her mom didn't want to go, fine. At this point, there was nothing Joss could think of to do to ease the bad feelings between them.

Dax and Shandie's big house was packed. All of Jace's siblings and their spouses were there. And so were Laila's sisters Annabel, Jasmine and Jordyn Leigh. Jace's mom and Pete were still in town, so they showed up, too. And then there was DJ and his family as well.

Joss visited with Claudia, who was all smiles over the coming wedding. Joss tried to take comfort in the way Jace's mom treated her. Claudia welcomed her into the Traub family with open arms. If only her own mom could be so accepting.

And if only the bleak doubts would quit dogging her.

She did worry, the more she thought about it, that Jace wasn't really ready for the life they planned together. If he *was* ready, how hard would it be for him to tell her he loved her and to actually mean it?

With half an ear, she listened to Dax and DJ talk about a couple of local crooks, Arthur Swinton and Jasper Fowler. The two men were in prison. They'd committed a series of crimes, including kidnapping Jace's sister, Rose Traub Anderson. The theory was that Swinton had nursed a grudge against the Traub family for decades because Dax and DJ's mom had turned him down flat when Swinton tried to put a move on her. DJ and Dax still couldn't quite believe that Swinton had gone off the deep end because their mom had turned him down. The more they discussed it, the more they agreed that Swinton's reaction to rejection had been way over the top, that there really had to be more to it than that.

Joss thought she could almost feel sorry for Arthur Swinton. It wasn't an easy thing to love someone who didn't love you back.

It was after midnight when she and Jace returned to the darkened apartment. The door to her mother's room was shut and no light bled out from beneath it.

They went to bed. Quietly. In order not to disturb the bitter, confused woman in the room down the hall. For the first time since they'd become lovers six nights before, they didn't make love. Joss just wasn't up for it, not with her disapproving mother right there in the apartment with them.

But Jace did pull her close and tuck her up nice and tight against him, wrapping that big, warm body of his all around her. Even with her doubts, she felt cherished. Cared for. She dropped off to sleep with a weary little sigh.

Her mom left after breakfast the next morning. RaeEllen and Joss shared an unenthusiastic final hug.

"I sent you a wedding invitation," Joss said. "I hope you'll come."

Her mother held herself stiffly in Joss's embrace. "Of course," she said in the somber tone of someone who'd just been asked to attend a funeral. "I'll be there."

During the first couple of days of the week that followed, Joss and Jace saw five new properties. Wednesday, they made an offer on eight green, rolling acres about two miles from town.

The house would need updating, but it had a little barn and a nice, big pasture for the horses Jace planned to bring up from his place in Texas. On Friday morning, a week and a day before their wedding, they signed the contract on their new home.

Jace took her out to the resort afterward to go riding. She was glad to see Cupcake. The sweet spotted horse seemed to recognize her. He nuzzled the side of her face and kept nudging her hand when she greeted him, urging her to stroke his long, noble forehead.

They rode up the mountain and then down into that valley on Clifton land, where they spread a saddle blanket under the cottonwoods and swam in the creek.

After they swam, they stretched out on the blanket and made out like a couple of horny kids. It was a beautiful day. For a while they lay there side-by-side, staring up at the blue sky, as the horses grazed nearby. They dozed—or at least Jace did.

Joss was wide awake. Her thoughts had turned, the way they did too often lately, to what was missing: his love. She watched a single fluffy cloud float across the blue expanse above and argued with herself, telling herself she really needed to get past this obsession with the L-word. Because, after all, it was just a word and what did a word matter?

"Is something wrong?" Jace asked softly.

"No, not a thing," she said. It was what she'd told him two other times in the past week, when he'd asked if she had something on her mind.

There was no point in going into it again. She loved him. He didn't have a clue what love was. What else was there to say?

Jace waited till they got back to the stables to tell her that he'd bought Cupcake for her.

She threw her arms around him and kissed him long and hard, right there in front of the gaping stable hand. Jace was such a great guy. The best.

Even if he didn't love her.

Even if she kept trying not to worry that someday he would leave her, the way her dad had left her mom.

The next week seemed to fly by. One moment it was Monday and they were making the arrangements for the various inspections at the Hitching Post and on their eight acres of land.

And then suddenly, it was Friday. The day before the wedding.

RaeEllen arrived late in the afternoon. She was actually smiling when Joss opened the door to her.

"Hello, Jocelyn." She held out her arms.

"Mom." Joss made herself smile in return. She acquiesced to the offered hug.

RaeEllen wheeled in her suitcase. "Where's Jason?"

Joss shut the door. "He's out at the new property we bought, following the inspector around. He should be back in an hour or so to say hi. And then he's off to the resort. His brothers and stepdad are throwing him a bachelor party. Tonight it will be just the two of us." Please God, they would get through it without any big scenes. "He'll stay over at his brother Jackson's house. Kind of a nod to tradition. I won't see him till I'm walking down the aisle to meet him tomorrow."

Her mother took her hand.

Joss quelled the urge to jerk away. "Mom, I want this to be a nice evening. Please."

And then her mother said something absolutely impossible. "I've had some time to think about my behavior, Jocelyn. It's been…a lonely time since I left here two weeks ago. And slowly, I've had to admit that I have been losing you, pushing you away by trying to tell you how to live your life. I've had to start facing a few not-so-pretty things about myself. You are the one shining, beautiful thing I've done in all my life. And I've been trying to tear you down."

Joss wasn't certain she'd heard right. "Um. You, um… huh?"

Her mom put her other hand on top of Joss's, so she held Joss's hand between both of hers. "You were right," she said. "It was all about me and what happened with your father. I never trusted a man after him. Not for years and years. And then, finally, I let myself believe that one man could be all right."

"Kenny…"

"Yes." RaeEllen gave a tight little nod. "I couldn't stand to admit that I'd been wrong again. I convinced you to stay with him when you were having second thoughts instead of really listening and trying to understand what was bothering you about your relationship with him. And then I did it again, I refused to hear you when you told me that Kenny betrayed you. I lost sight of what really matters, of what my real job is as your mother now that you're an adult. I treated you like a misbehaving child instead of respecting your decisions and offering my support."

"Oh, Mom..."

"But I want to make things right with you. I want you to know that from now on, I'm not making everything all about me. From now on, I *am* on your side, Jocelyn. It's *your* choice who you marry. And Jason seems like a fine young man. I support you in your choice. I hope—no. I'm *sure* that you and Jason will be very happy together."

Joss's throat locked up and her eyes brimmed. She managed to croak a second time, "Oh, Mom..."

And then they were both reaching out, grabbing each other close, holding on so very tight....

"I love you, honey," her mother said. "I love you and I...support you. Please forgive me for being such a blind, hopeless fool."

When Jace let himself in the apartment an hour later, he heard laughter coming from the kitchen. Joss said something. And then she laughed.

The sound echoed down inside him, warm. Sexy. Good. No one had a laugh like Joss's.

And then another voice answered Joss. Her mother's voice, but lighter than before. Happier. RaeEllen laughed, too.

He followed the cheerful sounds and stood in the doorway to the long, cozy kitchen.

"Jace!" Joss came to him, kissed him.

And then her mother came and gave him a hug and said it was good to see him. She actually seemed to mean it.

RaeEllen, it appeared, had seen the light, which was very good news. It had been so bad the last time she showed up that he'd been kind of dreading her reappearance. Joss had never told him the things her mother had said that afternoon when he'd left them together to have it out. But he knew they couldn't have been good. And he figured RaeEllen must have had a few choice words to say about him.

Sometimes, in the past two weeks, he would catch Joss watching him, a mournful look in her eyes. He figured her mother had filled her head with negative garbage about him, and about the two of them getting married. But when he asked her what was wrong, she said it was nothing.

He didn't believe that. Still, he didn't push her to bust to the truth. There was the whole love thing between them now and he didn't want to get into that again. He knew she wanted—needed—for him to say the words.

And he would. Hell, he *had.* But it hadn't worked out because she read him like a book and knew he didn't mean them.

How could he mean them? He'd told her what he thought of love. He didn't have any idea what love was. But he did want to marry her. He wanted *her*, damn it.

He didn't get why that couldn't be enough for her.

After tomorrow, he told himself, once they were married, things would smooth out. Hey, look what had happened with RaeEllen. She'd had a little time to think over the situation and decided to get with the program and be happy that her daughter had found someone she wanted to make a life with.

It would be the same with Joss. She would see how well things worked out. And she would be happy. He was counting on that.

Jace took a seat at the table and hung around a while. RaeEllen poured him some coffee and he watched the two women bustling between the stove and the counter, putting their dinner together. When he got up to go, Joss followed him to the door.

She whispered, "In case you didn't notice, my mom's come around."

"I kind of had a feeling she might have."

"I still can't believe it. It's like a miracle."

"Hey." He smoothed that wildly curling cinnamon-shot hair of hers. "It's not all *that* surprising."

"It is to me."

"She loves you," he said, uttering the dangerous word without stopping to think about it. "She's figured out that she needs to be on your side."

"Love..." Joss glanced away and then she was tipping her face up to him again, putting on a big smile. "Have fun." She kissed him.

He left feeling strangely regretful. As though he should have said something he hadn't.

As though he'd missed his chance somehow.

The bachelor party went on until after two. It was great, hanging with his brothers and his cousins, getting to know the two Traubs from Rust Creek Falls. Forrest was thirty-one, an Iraq veteran slowly recovering from a serious leg injury. His brother, Clay, was twenty-nine, a single father. They—and Jace—were the only unmarried men at the party. They both seemed like solid, down-to-earth dudes.

But there were a lot of toasts. And Forrest and Clay joined in every one. By the end of the evening, they were both wasted. Jace grinned to himself watching them.

He caught Jackson's eye and knew his brother was remembering how it had been back in June the year before, when Corey had his bachelor party over at the Hitching Post and Jace and Jackson had really tied one on. Jace hadn't slept at all the night of that party. He'd spent a few energetic hours with the one and only Theresa Duvall and then left her to rejoin his brother. He and Jackson had kept drinking right through Corey's wedding and the reception the next day. It hadn't been pretty. In fact, Jackson had started a brawl at the reception.

Jace doubted that the Rust Creek boys would pull any crap like that tomorrow. But he'd bet they would be nursing a matched pair of killer hangovers. Jace didn't envy them.

And he didn't miss the single life at all.

Ethan raised his glass—again. "To Jace, the last single maverick."

His brothers all laughed, in on the joke, remembering the way their long-lost dad use to call them his little mavericks.

Jace wondered what Joss and her mom were doing.

Which he supposed was pretty damn pitiful. It was only one night away from her.

Well, and then tomorrow. He wouldn't see her in the morning either. The wedding wasn't until five, so he'd be on his own for most of the day.

He really needed to buck up. It wasn't going to kill him to be away from her until the big moment when she came down the aisle to marry him.

In the dress she bought to marry that cheating SOB Kenny.

He didn't like that she would be wearing that damn dress. Every time he thought of it, it bugged him more.

But he hadn't known exactly how to tell her that he wanted her to choose something else. And now, well, it was a little late to do much about it.

She would be wearing that dress. Period. End of story.

He decided for about the hundredth time that he would forget how much he hated that damn dress.

At three in the morning, back at Jackson's place, he said goodnight to his brother, gave the mutt Einstein a scratch behind the ear and headed for the guest room.

It was lonely in there. He missed Joss, missed the way she tucked her round, perfect bottom up against him, how she took his arm and wrapped it around her, settling it in the sweet curve of her waist, before she went to sleep. He missed the little sounds she made when she was dreaming. Sometimes he wondered if he was getting whipped.

Because he was completely gone on her.

Every day, every hour, every time his damn heart beat, he got somehow more…attached to her.

And no. It wasn't love. He didn't know what love was. He was just a not-very-deep guy who'd finally found the right woman for him.

He wanted her with him.

And he would have her.

From tomorrow afternoon on.

At four the next afternoon, wearing his best tux, which he'd had sent up from Midland, Jace arrived at the resort. Lizzie and Laila had taken charge of decorating the small ballroom for the ceremony.

The room was beautiful, set up like a church chapel, with white folding chairs decked out in netlike white fabric, satin ribbons and flowers, a long satin runner for the aisle and a white flower-bedecked arch above the spot where he and Joss would say their vows. Tall vases on pedestals sprouting a variety of vivid flowers flanked the arch, stood at either end of the aisle and on either side of the two sets of wide double doors.

Jace had only Jackson standing up with him. And Joss hadn't chosen any bridesmaids; she wasn't even having anyone give her away. It was going to be short and sweet and simple, which was just fine with Jace. They would marry and head for the Rib Shack to celebrate.

And everything would be good between them. Everything would be great.

He hung around up by the white arch with Jackson and the nice pastor from the Community Church, waiting, nodding and waving at the guests as they entered. He smiled at Laila's single sisters Annabel, Jordyn Leigh and Jasmine. The three came in together, each in a pretty bright-colored summer dress. Forrest Traub limped in wearing his Sunday best, Clay right behind him. As Jace had expected, the Rust Creek Falls Traubs were looking a little green around the gills from partying too heartily the night before.

At five o'clock, almost every chair was taken. Lizzie cued the wedding march. Ma and Pete entered together down the aisle, arm-in-arm, and sat in the front row. RaeEllen came next, escorted by Ethan. He walked her to the front and she sat between him and Lizzie, who was already in her chair.

There was a strange, breath-held moment, when the wedding march played on and Jace's heart seemed to have lodged firmly in his throat and he stared up the aisle toward the small door on the far wall, suddenly scarily certain that Joss had changed her mind about the whole thing. That she'd lifted her white skirts for the second time and sprinted away from the small ballroom and him and the future they had promised they would share together.

But at last, the door opened. And there she was, more beautiful than ever, even if she was wearing that damn dreaded dress. She carried a big bouquet of orchids and daylilies, each exotic bloom more beautiful than the last.

She saw him, there beneath the flowered arch, waiting for her. And she gave him a secret, perfect, radiant smile. And then she started walking, slowly, the way brides always do. Step, pause. Step, pause. He wanted her to hurry. He wanted her beside him. Somehow, as he watched her coming to him, his throat opened up and his heart bounced back down into his chest where it belonged. And he could breathe again.

And still, slowly, so slowly, she came to him. His eyes drank her in and the strangest thing was happening. The craziest, wildest, most impossible thing. The thing that never happened to a shallow, good-time guy like him.

Light. It shone all around her. Golden and blinding, and he couldn't look away.

Why would he want to look away? It was one of those moments. A man like him might not understand it, but that didn't matter. What mattered was that Joss was coming to him, her big, brandy-brown eyes only for him, and there was a light all around her, a light coming from her. She was a beacon, *his* beacon. All he had to do was look for her. Find her.

Follow her light.

All at once, she was there. At his side. And she gave him her free hand and they turned to the nice pastor.

And Jace was *in* the light with her, a part of the light. Should that have freaked him out? Probably. But it didn't. He didn't mind it at all. In fact, it felt great. He knew that being in the light with Joss was exactly the place he was meant to be.

And the pastor started talking, saying the words of the marriage ceremony. Everything was magical and hushed and…more.

More than he'd ever known.

Better than he ever could have dreamed. It was all coming clear to him, all so simple.

And so right.

Until the pastor said, "If there be any man or woman who knows a reason why these two should not be joined in holy matrimony, let them speak now or forever after hold their peace."

And all at once, there was something going on at the entrance, by the twin sets of double doors. The light that held him and Joss was fading.

Joss gasped. And then she groaned. "Oh, no. Not Kenny…and Kimberly, too."

Jace turned toward the doors and saw the tall, fit-looking blond guy in the pricey khakis and the pale blue polo shirt.

"Jocelyn, I'm here," the guy said, noble-sounding as the hero in some old-time melodrama. "Don't do this. Forget that guy. We can work it out. Don't ruin our lives. I know there were…issues. I get that I blew it, but that was weeks ago. We need to get past all that garbage and you need to know that I love you and only you—and look." He gestured at the plump, pretty girl in the yellow sundress, who stood blinking uncomfortably at his side. "I brought Kimberly. She's here to tell you how sorry she is that she's made all this trouble." He jabbed at Kimberly with an elbow. "Tell her," he muttered. "Speak up and tell her now."

Kimberly burst into tears.

Kenny gaped. "Kimberly, what are you doing? Stop that!"

Kimberly cried all the harder. She let out a low wail and covered her eyes with her hands. Everyone in the ballroom was watching them, staring uncomfortably, the way people do when driving by car wrecks.

It was a bizarre moment, so strange that Jace wasn't as angry as he might have been at the sudden appearance of Joss's cheating ex, at the dousing of the golden light.

"Kimberly." Kenny actually took her shoulders and shook her. "Snap out of it. Remember? You're here to help."

"I caaaaan't. I just caaaan't," Kimberly wailed. She

jerked free of Kenny's grip and whirled to face the flower-decked arch and Joss and Jace standing in front of it. "Joss, I'm so sorry. But, you know, I'm *not* sorry. I've always loved Kenny and we've been seeing each other behind your back for the past six months now."

Kenny blinked and shook his perfectly groomed golden head. "Ahem, Kimberly." He tried to reach for her again but she jumped away. "Now, stop that." He cast a frantic glance at Joss again. "Joss, it's not true. I don't know what's gotten into her."

"But it *is* true," cried Kimberly.

"Of course it's not!" Kenny shouted. Then he caught himself. He lowered his voice and spoke out of the corner of his mouth. "You told me you would *help* me. You are not helping. This is not why I brought you here."

"Oh, Kenny, I know it's not. But I just can't stop myself. I'm sick of it, Kenny. Sick, sick, sick. Sick of the lies, sick of my part in this whole humiliating, ridiculous charade. I can see you for who you really are now. I know that you're not worth crap. And you know what? This, today? This does it. I'm through with you. Finished. And I'm glad for Joss. I'm smiling through my tears that my cousin got away without ruining her life and marrying you, you big butthead, creep-faced, yuppie dirtbag, you giant pile of designer-clad trash."

Kenny made a growling sound. "Why you skeevy little bitch…" His face the color of a ripe tomato, he went for Kimberly.

But Kimberly only grabbed a nearby vase of wedding flowers and hurled it at his head.

Kenny ducked.

The vase kept going until it smacked into the side of Forrest Traub's face. Flowers and water went flying.

"Hey!" Forrest lurched upward, trampling the boots of the cowboy sitting next to him.

"Watch it, buddy." The cowboy jumped to his feet and punched Forrest in the jaw. Forrest punched him back. The cowboy fell on the woman sitting next to him. She let out a scream, which caused the man on her other side to leap up and go after the cowboy.

In the meantime, Kenny was chasing Kimberly around the ballroom as Kimberly ran from him, sobbing and screaming and calling him all kinds of imaginative names.

At Jace's side, Joss made a low, sad little sound. "What a disaster…"

That spurred Jace to action. He'd had about enough, too. Kimberly had run down around the other end of the rows of chairs and started up on the far side, coming toward the flowered arch where Joss, Jace, Jackson and the pastor still stood.

Jace waited until Kimberly fled by him, then he stepped forward between the fleeing girl and Kenny. Kenny tried to sprint around him. Jace only slid to the side and blocked him again.

"Outta my way," Kenny huffed.

And Jace drew back his fist and laid the other man flat with one clean right to his perfect square jaw.

Jace stood over the jerk. "Don't get up until I say so."

The man in the polo shirt groaned and tested his jaw and glared up at Jace. But he didn't get up.

By then, the fight in the chairs had spread to every other short-tempered cowboy in attendance. There were more than a few of them, evidently. The men were fighting and the women were alternately shouting at them to stop and screaming "Look out!" and trying in lower voices to settle them all down.

Over by the double doors, Kimberly was still crying.

Melba Landry had gone to comfort her. Joss's cousin clung to Melba and drenched the old woman's flower-patterned purple church dress with an endless flood of desperate tears.

Melba was talking to her in low tones, soothing her, Jace had no doubt. And probably reminding her that there was peace in the Lord.

As quickly as it had started, the brawl wound down.

Things got quiet. Really quiet. The ballroom was in chaos, chairs overturned, vases spilled and shattered, wedding flowers torn and tattered, trampled underfoot. The guests all stood around, clothing askew, hair every which way, looking slightly stunned.

Jace turned to Joss.

But she wasn't there.

"Joss?" And then he spotted her.

She was over by the doors, not far from where Kimberly held on to Melba.

Joss met his eyes. And at that moment, there was no one else in that chair-strewn ballroom. Just him and Joss.

Her eyes shone bright with tears. She said, "This isn't going to work. I can't…" She ran out of words.

"I understand," he answered gently. And he did, though his heart seemed to shrivel to a wasted shell inside his chest. "You're right. It's all wrong."

She threw her bouquet. It sailed over the heads of several shell-shocked guests and into the arms of Annabel Cates, who caught it automatically to keep it from hitting her in the face.

And then, as he'd been secretly fearing she might do for the last couple of weeks now, Joss lifted her froth of skirts, whirled away from him and sprinted from the ballroom.

Chapter Fourteen

RaeEllen appeared at Jace's side. She glared down at Kenny. "Shame on you, Kenny Donovan."

Kenny groaned and started to rise. Jace gave him a look and he sank back to the floor.

RaeEllen turned to Jace. "You have to go after her."

Jace wrapped his arm around Joss's mom. "You okay, RaeEllen?"

Her hazel eyes were dark with concern. "Oh, Jason. I swear to you, I had nothing to do with this. I didn't say a word to Kenny—or Kimberly—about where or when you and Jocelyn were getting married."

Jace patted RaeEllen's shoulder. "I know you didn't. Joss told him, weeks ago, on the phone. She was just trying to get it through his fat head that she really was moving on with her life."

RaeEllen pressed her hand to her heart. "Oh, I just feel terrible about all this…."

"Not your fault," he reassured her. "You and Joss have worked things out. She knows you're on her side."

Jackson, his wife beside him by then, asked, "What do we do now?"

It was a good question. "Hey, everyone," Jace called out loud enough to carry to the back of the ballroom. "Looks like the wedding isn't happening. But there's a party waiting for all of you at the Rib Shack. I want you to head on over there and have yourselves a great time."

People exchanged anxious glances.

Then Clay Traub said, "Great idea, Jace. Come on, everyone, let's head for the Rib Shack."

The guests began filing out.

Jace sent a lowering glance down at Kenny. "*You're* not invited. In fact, you can get the hell out—of the clubhouse, of the resort, of the town of Thunder Canyon. Get out and don't come back. Do it now."

Kenny didn't argue. He dragged himself upright and staggered out.

Jace's brothers, his sister, their spouses and Ma and Pete stuck around to straighten up the ballroom. Kimberly and Melba stayed to help, too, as did RaeEllen. It didn't take all that long. Twenty minutes after they started picking up the chairs, they all left together, on their way to the Rib Shack.

All except Jace. He wasn't going to his own nonreception. Not without his runaway bride.

He found her where he knew she would be—in the Lounge, with a margarita in front of her. She'd taken off her veil and let her hair down. She'd also ordered him a whisky on the rocks.

He almost grinned. "You have a lot of faith in me."

"Yeah," she replied softly, her eyes getting misty again. "I do." She patted the stool beside her. "Have a seat."

He eased her big, fat skirt out of the way and took the stool she offered him.

She picked up her drink and he lifted his. They tapped their glasses together and drank.

When she set hers down, she said, "Got something to say to me?"

"I do." He thought about the golden light, the magic that had happened back there in the ballroom. But then he decided that maybe it wasn't magic after all.

Maybe it was only the most natural, down-to-earth thing in the world. A man seeing what mattered, seeing it fully for the very first time.

A man recognizing the right woman. *His* woman.

And knowing absolutely, without even the faintest shadow of a doubt that she was the only one for him. That he knew what love was after all.

Because he loved her.

"I like you, Joss."

She almost rolled her eyes, but not quite. "There'd better be more."

"There is."

"I'm listening."

"I like you. I want you. You…light up my life. You're the only woman in the world for me. I want the life we planned, want to be your partner in the Hitching Post. I want our eight acres and the house that needs work and the horses and the dog we haven't found yet. I want your children to be *my* children. I want to sleep with you in my arms every night and wake up in the morning with you beside me."

Now her adorable mouth was trembling. "Oh, Jace…"

"There's more."

"Tell me. Please."

"What I *don't* want is to lie to you—or myself—anymore. I not only like you. I *love* you. I'm *in* love with you. It's real and it's forever as far as I'm concerned."

"Oh, Jace…" Her eyes, unabashedly tear-wet now, gleamed like dark jewels.

He dared to reach out to touch her cheek, her shining hair. And he whispered, prayerfully, "Damn if I don't finally get what all the shouting's about when it comes to love and marriage and a lifetime together. It's *you*, Joss. You've shown me that. You've shown me love. I want to marry you. More than anything. I want to be with you for the rest of my life. And I have to tell you…"

"Yes? What? Anything, you know that."

"What I *don't* want is to marry you in that dress you bought to marry Kenny Donovan in—no matter how drop-dead gorgeous you look in the damn thing."

She laughed then, that low, rich, husky laugh that belonged only to her. "Okay." She offered her hand. "Yes, I'll marry you. And I promise I won't wear this dress when I do it."

He skipped the handshake and reached for her, gently sliding his fingers around the back of her neck, under the splendid, rich fall of her cinnamon-shot hair. And he kissed her. "I love you, Joss."

"And I love you. So much. I'm so glad…that you can finally say it."

He cradled the side of her face, oblivious to the bartender who watched them, wearing a dazed sort of smile, from down at the other end of the bar. "I'm sorry," Jace whispered. "So sorry I was such an idiot. So sorry I hurt you…."

"It's okay now."

"I'll say it again. I love you. I'll say it a hundred times a day."

She laughed then. "Oh, I'm so glad. I *was* a little worried."

"I know you were."

"But I'm not anymore. You have put my fears to rest, Jason Traub. You have given me everything—more that I ever dreamed of. And you know what? I love you with all my heart and it means so much to me to be able to tell you so at last without freaking you out. To know that you love me, too." She raised her glass again. "To love."

He touched his glass to hers. "And forever."

"To the Hitching Post. And the house and the horses and the dog."

"And the rowdy kids."

"And to us, Jace."

"Yes, Joss. To us, most of all."

Not much later, they joined the party that was supposed to have been their reception. They danced every dance, enjoyed the great food Shane Roark had prepared for them, fed each other big, delicious chunks of Lizzie's fabulous cake.

It was a beautiful evening. One of the best.

And after all the guests went home, they took the elevator upstairs to the Honeymoon Suite, theirs for that special nonwedding night, courtesy of Thunder Canyon Resort.

They made love. It was amazing.

Better than ever. So good that when they were finished, they made love again. And again after that.

The next morning at a little before seven, Joss woke alone in the big pillow-top bed.

She sat up. "Jace?"

And then she saw him—in the chair by the bed, dressed in a beautiful lightweight suit, holding a handful of wildflowers. He held them out to her. "Marry me, Jocelyn Marie. Marry me today."

She didn't hesitate. She got up, put on a pretty summer dress, took the flowers from him and off they went, stopping only to collect his parents from their suite and her mother from the apartment over the Mountain Bluebell Bakery.

At the Community Church, the nice minister was willing to be persuaded to perform the wedding ceremony that hadn't happened the day before. And there in the pretty white chapel on that sunny Sunday morning well before the regular service, Joss and Jace said their vows.

And when the pastor announced, "You may kiss the bride," Jason Traub knew that he'd finally found what he'd been looking for. He took his bride in his arms and he kissed her.

And when he lifted his head, he whispered, "I love you, Joss Traub. Forever."

"Forever," she echoed.

It was a great moment. The best in his life so far.

For a while there he really had been the last single maverick, wondering where he'd missed out, envious of his brothers and his sister, who had found what they were looking for, had all gotten married and settled down.

He'd felt left out of something important, and left behind as well. That was all changed now by the woman in his arms. He was part of something bigger now.

The last single maverick was single no more.

* * * * *

COMING NEXT MONTH from Harlequin® Special Edition®

AVAILABLE JULY 24, 2012

#2203 PUPPY LOVE IN THUNDER CANYON

Montana Mavericks: Back in the Saddle

Christyne Butler

An intense, aloof surgeon meets his match in a friendly librarian who believes that emotional connections can heal—and she soon teaches him that love is the best medicine!

#2204 THE DOCTOR AND THE SINGLE MOM

Men of Mercy Medical

Teresa Southwick

Dr. Adam Stone picked the wrong place to rent. Or maybe just the wrong lady to rent from. Jill Beck is beloved—and protected—by the entire town. One wrong move with the sexy single mom could cost him a career in Blackwater Lake, Montana—and the chance to fill up the empty place inside him.

#2205 RILEY'S BABY BOY

Reunion Brides

Karen Rose Smith

Feuding families make a surpise baby and even bigger challenges. Are Brenna McDougall and Riley O'Rourke ready for everything life has in store for them? Including a little surpise romance?

#2206 HIS BEST FRIEND'S WIFE

Gina Wilkins

How much is widowed mom Renae Sanchez willing to risk for a sexy, secretive man from her past...a man she once blamed for her husband's death?

#2207 A WEEK TILL THE WEDDING

Linda Winstead Jones

Jacob Tasker and Daisy Bell think they are doing the right thing when they pretend to still be engaged for the sake of his sick grandmother. But as their fake nuptials start leading to real love, they find out that granny may have a few tricks up her old sleeve!

#2208 ONE IN A BILLION

Home to Harbor Town

Beth Kery

A potential heiress—the secret baby of her mother's affair—is forced by the will to work with her nemesis, a sexy tycoon, to figure out the truth about her paternity, and what it means for the company of which she now owns half!

Angie Bartlett and Michael Robinson are friends. And following the death of his wife, Angie's best friend, their bond has grown even more. But that's all there is...right?

Read on for an exciting excerpt of WITHIN REACH by Sarah Mayberry, available August 2012 from Harlequin® Superromance®.

"HEY. RIGHT ON TIME," Michael said as he opened the door.

The first thing Angie registered was his fresh haircut and that he was clean shaven—a significant change from the last time she'd visited. Then her gaze dropped to his broad chest and the skintight black running pants molded to his muscular legs. The words died on her lips and she blinked, momentarily stunned by her acute awareness of him.

"You've cut your hair," she said stupidly.

"Yeah. Decided it was time to stop doing my caveman impersonation."

He gestured for her to enter. As she brushed past him she caught the scent of his spicy deodorant. He preceded her to the kitchen and her gaze traveled across his shoulders before dropping to his backside. Angie had always made a point of not noticing Michael's body. They were friends and she didn't want to know that kind of stuff. Now, however, she was forcibly reminded that he was a *very* attractive man.

Suddenly she didn't know where to look.

It was then that she noticed the other changes—the clean kitchen, the polished dining table and the living room free of clutter and abandoned clothes.

"Look at you go." Surely these efforts meant he was rejoining life.

HSREXP0812

He shrugged, but seemed pleased she'd noticed. "Getting there."

They maintained eye contact and the moment expanded. A connection that went beyond the boundaries of their friendship formed between them. Suddenly Angie wanted Michael in ways she'd never felt before. *Ever*.

"Okay. Let's get this show on the road," his six-year-old daughter, Eva, announced as she marched into the room.

Angie shook her head to break the spell and focused on Eva. "Great. Looking forward to a little light shopping?"

"Yes!" Eva gave a squeal of delight, then kissed her father goodbye.

Angie didn't feel 100 percent comfortable until she was sliding into the driver's seat.

Which was dumb. It was nothing. A stupid, odd bit of awareness that meant *nothing*. Michael was still Michael, even if he was gorgeous. Just because she'd tuned in to that fact for a few seconds didn't change anything.

Does Angie's new awareness mark a permanent shift in their relationship? Find out in WITHIN REACH by Sarah Mayberry, available August 2012 from Harlequin® Superromance®.

HSREXP0812